BEST
EROTIC
·ROMANCE
2013

BEST

EROTIC

ROMANCE

2013

Edited by
KRISTINA WRIGHT

Foreword by
SASKIA WALKER

CLEiS
PRESS

Published in the United States by Cleis Press Inc., 2246 Sixth Street, Berkeley, California 94710.

Printed in the United States.
Cover design: Scott Idleman/Blink
Cover photograph: Jean-Claude Marlaud/Getty Images
Text design: Frank Wiedemann
First Edition.
10 9 8 7 6 5 4 3 2 1

Trade paper ISBN: 978-1-57344-903-8
E-book ISBN: 978-1-57344-920-5

CONTENTS

FOREWORD

Saskia Walker

Erotic Romance, how do I love thee? Let me count the ways...

Ah, curling up with a hot and steamy erotic romance—there are few more delicious pleasures. These days I rarely read a romance that doesn't include the erotic element. When the eroticism and the emotional aspects of the story entwine it's simply the best kind of story for me, and that goes for many other readers too. Sexuality is part of human nature, so it doesn't seem right to leave it out of a story about developing relationships. Whilst erotic scenes are rewarding reads in themselves, they resonate most when they are an integral part of the characters' falling in love and expressing their emotions to each other. Not only that, but the most basic as well as the deepest of human emotions and experiences can be found and portrayed in the act of physical love. Moments of conflict, too, can be profoundly moving during intimacy. As readers we partake of that adventure. We understand the obstacles that have to be conquered. We feel the risk, fear and ecstasy of falling in love, and we thrill at the heady pleasure of decadent sex—all those things that call to the wilder side of our souls.

We haven't always had this subgenre. When I began reading romance many, many years ago, I loved the books, simply couldn't get enough. I jumped aboard the protagonist's journey eagerly, savoring the ride. But when the bedroom door closed me out it was a big letdown. It felt wrong. I felt deprived. The hero's broad shoulders had loomed closer and I would be as breathless with expectation as the heroine. When that was followed by a description of the flames in the fireplace then a cut to the heroine's postcoital happiness in his arms, I knew I had been cheated of an essential part of the relationship unfolding. I used to flick the pages back and forth, seriously convinced that someone had torn some pages out of the book, because some-thing was definitely missing and it just wasn't right. The bait was set in my blood. I wanted those intimate scenes because I knew they would make the rest of the story vibrant and whole.

Thankfully, over the last two decades the bedroom door has not only been left wide open, it has frequently been rattled off its hinges by the passionate intensity on the pages. Erotic romance as a genre has grown in leaps and bounds. Over the last five years in particular we've had access to a wealth of reading mate-rial to satisfy our desire for these kinds of stories. In 2012, erotic romance books topped the bestseller charts and stayed there. For readers this is great news, and there are some terrific erotic romance writers out there—and these writers can take us right into the heart of a relationship, their talent as wordsmiths clev-erly illustrating how evocative the physical aspect can be. In the short-story form in particular, a carefully crafted glimpse into the erotic romance is a thrilling experience, a window into the most exciting and satisfying of relationships. If readers witness the romance overcome difficult circumstances and flourish during the erotic scenes it makes for both a steamy and emotionally fulfilling read. That's what you have here in your hands.

Erotic Romance, how do I love thee? Let me count the ways...

Here in this collection you have seventeen ways. Read the stories of writers who perfectly understand the intersection of the physical and the emotional. Savor and enjoy.

Saskia Walker
The wilds of West Yorkshire, England

INTRODUCTION:
CAN'T GET ENOUGH

Love. The word conjures up a variety of images, from sappy to cynical. Love is the heart's calling, a need for connection with another soul.

So what happens when love meets sex? Erotic love is that delicious blend of hearts and minds and bodies, a combination of sweet and dirty, romantic and sexy. Sex by itself—hot, steamy, sensual sex—is one of the best things this life has to offer. But then, so is love. First love, new love, renewed love; love that has stood the test of time, love that has conquered every obstacle. It doesn't matter if it's a new relationship, such as Jeanette Grey's yoga-bound characters in "Teach Me," or a long-term relationship like Dominic Santi's happily (and lustily) married couple in "Kiss of Peace"— the combination of sex and love is incendiary.

Best Erotic Romance 2013 is not about fantasy love affairs. It's not about perfect bodies having perfect sex and being perfectly in love. These stories are about the messiness, the *screwed-uppedness*, of love and lust. These are stories about people you might know, people who might even be you. People whose bodies aren't perfect, whose words are not always right or kind, people who fall in love and have sex when and where they can even when it's not always easy or convenient or even wise.

Love is messy and complicated—except when it's not. But even when it's right, even when the stars have aligned to bring two people together who are perfect for each other, there are obstacles. There are children and careers and birth-control issues and homes to renovate and scheduling problems and forgotten anniversaries and, and, and...there's always something to throw a wrench in the works and drag two people apart instead of pulling them together and into bed. But they make it work and, eventually, they find their way to that bed. Or the couch. Or the wall. Or the yard. Or the car. They take each other's hand and they *find a way* to be together in all the ways that matter. For today, for now, forever. That's what happens when love and sex come together. Hopeless, maddening, passionate, sexy love.

The stories in this book are a promise. A promise that erotic love does exist, that it is real and powerful and all encompassing. A promise that, once found, it can and does last. For a lifetime, if you're lucky. A promise to you, dear reader, that these stories exist because we, the writers, believe in erotic love. Believe it, live it, write it—and cherish it, just like you do.

May you find the love you're looking for—or keep the love you already have.

Kristina Wright
In love in Virginia

KISS AND MAKE UP

Heidi Champa

"Come on, Ophelia. How long are you going to stay mad at me?"

I didn't answer him. I was too angry to give in to him just yet. I was intent on staying mad for a lot longer. He had messed up, and I wasn't about to let him off the hook. A ten-year anniversary doesn't come around every year. And he had forgotten. Not even so much as a card. I'd gone all out of course. I'd bought him a vintage watch and had it engraved with the date of our wedding. It took me months to find it and once I did, I couldn't wait to see Ted's face when he opened the box.

Ted had never been the most romantic guy, but I fully expected after ten years together, he'd be able to come up with something special for us. Imagine my surprise when I presented the gift during the elaborate meal I'd created and saw his face drop when I said the words *Happy Anniversary.* That had been two days ago, and I was still seething. He'd tried everything to get me to talk to him, but I hadn't said more than hello and good-bye to him. I wanted to get over it, but I didn't know how. Ted, it seemed, was trying again and I was going to do my best to resist his latest lame attempt to get me to forgive him.

"The silent treatment. That's fine. I'll just have to get you to talk to me another way."

He let his hands slip around my back and I felt his body press slowly against me. He leaned his head down toward me and I closed my eyes. His lips were so close to mine, I could feel the softness of his breath right in front of me. The lightest brush of his lips hit mine, and my breath caught in my throat. He held his lips there, not going any farther, barely touching. It was torture.

"Still not going to say anything? I guess I'm not as convincing as I thought." He kept his tease going. I let him move us forward. His hand slid up to my neck and I felt his fingers going through my hair. His mouth was right over mine, our mouths nearly mingling. I was still angry, really angry, but there was a small part of me that wanted to devour him right there in the kitchen.

"Well, I guess if you're not going to give in, I'm going to have to get tough." I was just about to laugh out loud at his assertion, when I felt his hand steal under my ass, and he hitched me up to the countertop without much effort. I sat in front of him, my legs locking behind his back without a conscious thought. His mouth moved to the soft lines of my neck, his lips setting small fires all over my skin. My hands traipsed over his hair, keeping him close to me. I breathed deep, realizing how I'd missed his smell. He had only spent one night on the couch. I resisted letting my own mouth explore his skin. I desperately wanted to kiss him, but I was trying to hold my ground. He pushed my hair back from my face and stared into my eyes.

"You are so beautiful, you know that?"

I tried to remain unmoved, but I felt myself blush. The heat of my face was nothing compared to my body, which was now practically on fire. I tried to push him back from the counter, but he just grabbed my hands. Before I could stop him, he was pulling me down the hallway to our bedroom. He walked backward right to the bed and sat down. His large hands in mine, he pulled me onto his lap.

"Come on, I said I was sorry. Aren't you going to forgive me? Please, pretty please. I know I've been a bad boy, but I want to make it up to you."

I didn't say a word. Maybe I was being unfair. After all, why should I punish myself for his mistakes? Instead of accepting his apology, I just straddled him. My legs wrapping around his waist, I kissed him deeply, rocking slightly on his lap. I reached for the hem of his shirt, pulling it up and over his head. I felt his bare chest with my hands, the heat coming off his skin in waves. My blouse and bra were off, ending up in a pile with the other clothes. He stopped, looking at my breasts in the dying daylight. His tongue flicked over my collarbone, dropping kisses down to my breasts. His fingers teased me, pulling my flesh into tight peaks, while his mouth came and went, only making me want it more. I arched my back, but he went on with his game. Until I started grinding myself against his growing cock. He then became much more generous with his affection. He looked up at me with his big puppy-dog eyes and pleaded with me once more.

"God, honey. I'm so sorry. Do you forgive me? Say you forgive me."

He moved right back to my breasts, not waiting for my response. The heat of his mouth on my nipple made me turn to jelly inside, while on the surface my body tensed with each sucking kiss. Before I knew it, he had flipped me on my back, resuming his torture of my hard nipples with his hands and mouth. I lay on the bed, helpless, letting him slowly circle each nipple with his tongue, his actions drawing me closer and closer to losing my mind. Then he started sinking lower, his mouth teasing and tickling down my stomach until I was trembling under his lips. I felt his long fingers tracing over the light fabric of my panties, running aimlessly about, avoiding what I really wanted him to touch.

The lightest pressure of his fingers made me heat up inside. I moved my hips in circles, enjoying the barest of touches. But I wanted more. I wanted those panties off; wanted his mouth on me. All that stood between us were the small black cotton panties he rubbed me through.

"You want them off, don't you?"

"Yeah." It was the first word I had managed since we started.

"Say, you accept my apology. Say you forgive me."

"Please, Ted. Please take them off."

"Not until you say it."

"Okay, okay. I forgive you. God, Ted. I forgive you. Please, please take them off now."

He hooked his fingers through the waistband, and the flimsy fabric slid down past my ankles. But he didn't go right back to my now-bare flesh. He was half on top of me, kissing me deeply on the mouth. His fingers danced over my taut nipple, barely grazing it. His hands seemed so big gripping my hips, pulling me close. My hands cradled his face, as I tried to hold on to the moment for as long as I could. I ran my finger over his mouth, and he caught it between his lips, sucking it in to his mouth. My stomach rolled over, and a new wash of heat ran through me. His face dropped from my hands, and he kissed down my neck to the sweep of my collarbone. Every inch of my skin caught fire, each little kiss and lick starting a new blaze. I clawed at his hair, urging him forward, pushing him farther down my body.

Ted would not be rushed. His mouth again latched on to my nipple, sucking it deep into his mouth, flicking it over and over with his tongue. Arching my back, I tried to get more. All I could think was that I needed more. More of anything that Ted wanted to give to me. The heat of his mouth was joined by his slow, tracing fingers moving up my thigh. I could feel the gentle tremble of my leg under his touch, every time he got nearer to my pussy. He seemed to be purposefully avoiding my most sensitive skin, teasing me with little touches everywhere else. He pushed my legs apart and I felt his fingers moving closer and closer to my cunt. Moans were escaping my throat as his mouth moved back and forth over my nipples, teasing one and then the other until I was ready to scream.

"Ted, I can't take much more of this."

"Do you really forgive me?"

"You are killing me."

"That isn't what I asked."

"Yes. Yes. I told you I forgive you. Now fuck me, please."

His mouth covered mine, stopping any more words from getting out. His finger had finally found my slick heat, and my hard clit was sliding under his soft touch. The small circles teased my clit until I found my hips moving along, trying to get Ted to go faster. But he kept going at the maddeningly slow pace, his eyes watching my face.

His finger slipped down past my clit and entered me, opening my pussy up for the first time. I gasped, closing my eyes tight. The flat of his palm grazed my clit, with each slide in and out.

"Open your eyes. Please, Ophelia, open your eyes."

I could barely stand it, but I did. His green eyes shone back at me, intense and sparkling.

"Ted, please, I need you."

He kissed me, hard and probing, all his energy filling me.

Without missing a beat, he lowered his face, sweeping kisses over my quivering hips and down to my open thighs. I felt his breath between my legs and his fingers caressing my lips, sweeping over me. He was just looking at me, taking me in while I was writhing, waiting for his mouth to touch me. I felt the tip of his tongue gently touch my clit, and I felt like my mind was going to come apart. His gentle sweeping strokes covered my pussy, teasing my sensitive skin until I was shaking and clawing at the sheets. The long fingers that I had fallen in love with so long ago were finally touching me, spreading me open, filling my tight pussy, pleasing me. The sensation was so intense, I didn't know if I could handle much more.

He kept slowing, teasing me, tasting me, urging my desire forward, pushing me closer to the edge. His fingertip swirled the smallest circles over my clit. I gasped at his masterful touch, the pressure just enough to thrill me but not enough to make me come. I felt two fingers surround my clit and slide up and back, causing a fresh surge of heat to rush right to my pussy. His impossibly long finger slid inside me, my walls gripping him, pulling him deeper.

"God, you are such a pushover. I would never have forgiven me if I were you. Lord knows I don't deserve it."

I could hear the laugh in his voice, and I would have wanted to smack him, if it didn't feel so good. After that, he stopped talking and went back to using all his weapons against me. I had taken as much as I could, and I wanted to give him something in return. I grabbed at him, pulling him up my body until we were again face-to-face. His kiss tasted like me, his lips hot with my wet pussy. It was amazing.

"So, you think you are off the hook, huh?"

"Well, yeah."

I rolled him onto his back and straddled him quickly.

"We'll see who's laughing in a minute."

I ran my hands over his chest, feeling every inch of tight muscle and the light smattering of hair that covered his chest. I ran my thumbs over his tight little nipples, smirking at the hitch it caused in his breath. I leaned down and kissed his chest, smelling him, tasting him with my tongue. Licking tiny flicks over his nipple, I grabbed it lightly with my teeth, and he put a hand to my head. I went about torturing his nipples a little longer, letting his moans make me even hotter. But I wanted more. His flat stomach beckoned to me and I let myself slide down his body. Kissing his navel, I felt his hard cock resting right between my tits. I let it drag over my soft skin, feeling it pulse and shake at the contact. It jerked forward, trying to get my attention. I smiled up at him; his eyes were glassy and fuzzy with need. Keeping his gaze on me, I let my tongue fall gently out of my mouth, and let the smallest lick move across the head.

"Are you really sorry?"

"Yes. God, yes."

"And you'll never do it again?"

"I promise. Please, Ophelia. I promise."

I wouldn't let him look away as I wrapped my lips around him, taking the soft velvety plum head between my wet lips. His gasp shot straight to my pussy, sending heat through me. I sucked him gently, until his eyes finally closed and his head thrust back into the pillow. Slowly I licked my way down the underside of his cock, flicking and gently sucking the sensitive ridge. Licking my way back up, I wrapped my mouth around him again, and let his cock sink deeper into my throat.

"Oh, god, Ophelia, now you're killing me."

I let the vibration of my stifled giggle buzz against him, and he let out a sharp moan. I took him deeper still into my throat, and his fingers stoked my neck, wrapping themselves in my hair.

My persistent sucking was driving him mad. The beautiful cut of his hips rested beneath my hands, the trembling I felt now passed on to him. He didn't let me go on much longer. Moving me gently up, he kissed me so hard I thought I would never catch my breath. Every time I thought he was finished with my mouth, he kissed me again, our tongues plunging, tracing, finding new places to go. I was above him, his cock resting mere inches from my dripping wet pussy.

"I love you, Ophelia. I promise I'll never be a jerk again."

"Sure you will. It's one of my favorite things about you. You can't go changing now. I love you too, Ted."

His name was barely out of my mouth when I felt the thick tip of his cock settle between my waiting cunt lips. He eased me down onto him, slowly inching me closer and closer to his body. When he slipped in to the hilt, I rested on his lap, unable to move. I thought my body was going to come apart. His hands wrapped around my hips, gently rocking me forward and back. Finally, my mind returned and I slid up and down his cock, feeling the sweet, deep pull of him with every stroke. I couldn't look away from his eyes. His hands freed my hips and roamed my body, touching off electric shocks with each pass. I was so deliciously full; his cock stretching me open, hitting deeper with each thrust. He pulled me forward to devour my mouth with his sweet kisses, taking my mouth over and over. My clit was rubbing against his body, and I swirled my hips around in a circle as he plunged into me.

I felt my body tightening, every muscle building with tension and pleasure. His thumbs rolled over my nipples, the tight flesh barely able to take much more. My body was shaking, and I felt my orgasm building in me, deep and powerful. Ted let his thumb drop lower, and I felt it stroke over my warm, wet clit, and I exploded. I cried out violently, gripping Ted's cock deep inside me, contracting around him. I filled the silence of his room with my voice, releasing the pleasure that had been building. I rode against him, letting my body rise and fall again and again, as pleasure seemed to be coming in never ending waves. Ted's hands dug deep valleys into my hips, and I felt his cock growing inside me as he grunted out his own orgasm, just as mine was coming to an end.

We collapsed together, spent. I rolled off of Ted, my body succumbing to exhaustion. I felt like I couldn't move even if I wanted to. Ted wrapped his arms around me, pulling me into the safety of his embrace.

"Happy anniversary, baby."

"Maybe next year, you'll remember."

"Why would I want to do that? Getting punished is too much fun."

WAITING FOR ILYA

Teresa Noelle Roberts

"I'm in the kitchen," Tom called, as Stacy walked in the door. "The steaks just went on."

She hurried to the kitchen, tossing her purse onto a chair in the living room in passing. Her well-thumbed copy of *Parenting Your Internationally Adopted Child* fell out and hit the floor, but she figured she'd pick it up later. After all, she'd just finished reading it for the third time on the bus home, and excited as she was about Ilya, she didn't need to start reading for the fourth time right this moment.

Two glasses of red wine perched on the shiny new kitchen counter. Tom was leaning against it, shirtless under a dark green apron that brought out the green in his hazel eyes.

Stacy took a second to stare appreciatively. Busy as they'd been, she hadn't taken enough time lately to appreciate how hot and sexy her husband was—although she supposed that wasn't a terribly motherly thought and she should definitely work at thinking like a mom. "You must have gotten home early tonight. What's the occasion?"

"Do I need an occasion to open a bottle of wine and make a nice dinner?" Tom brandished the corkscrew dramatically.

"I guess not." She hoped she didn't sound suspicious, but she was certainly surprised. They'd been focusing so much of their energy on the adoption and on getting the house ready for Ilya, and putting so much money into the house and the multiple trips to Russia that wine and steak *did* feel like an occasion.

"It's Friday night." Tom set the corkscrew on the counter. "I figure we're past due for a date night, especially since we won't have a lot of chances for date nights pretty soon because we'll have a son." He grinned like he wasn't much older than five-year-old Ilya himself. "Just three more weeks until we bring Ilya home! Isn't that enough of an occasion—that and the fact that I love you madly?" He drew her into his arms and a kiss.

As the kiss blossomed on Stacy's lips, she remembered how Friday nights—and Tuesdays and Thursdays, for that matter— used to be. They hadn't planned on buying a house yet, not until the adoption was completed and Ilya had settled into life with his new family, but this one had been such a deal, and had such a big, beautiful yard, perfect for a child to run around in and get healthy after his rough start in life, that they jumped on it even though it needed "a little work."

They hadn't comprehended how much work, on top of the time and emotional energy going into the adoption.

They needed this night. They really did.

But they were on a timetable. Parents couldn't afford to be selfish. "We were going to work on Ilya's room tonight," Stacy said in a small but persistent voice. They hadn't expected the adoption to be finalized before September, but a few days ago they'd gotten the good news they could return to Moscow in less than a month to bring home the little boy they'd come to love over the course of their visits to Russia—a delightful, yet daunting surprise. "He deserves a room of his own. Though I suppose he might be happier in our room for a while," she reflected. "After all, he's slept in a dormitory with a bunch of other kids his whole life. Being alone at night on top of all the other changes might be too scary."

"All the more reason to enjoy tonight. Having a child will be a big change for us, especially if he starts out sleeping in our room. A wonderful change, but it's going to cut down on date nights, not to mention spontaneous kinky sex. Better enjoy those things while we can."

Anger surged through her, protective fury for the child who was theirs in everything but the paperwork. Was Tom already complaining about parenthood when Ilya wasn't even with them yet?

As quickly as the anger rose, it subsided. Stacy knew these feelings were just a cover for her own fears. Tom had a good point. Even now, just working to get the house ready for their child, she'd been stressed and more than a bit horny, feeling like she shouldn't take the time to fool around with her husband, but definitely missing it. But wouldn't taking a night off for themselves, when Ilya was arriving so soon and the house was still a shambles, be perilously close to saying they weren't ready for Ilya—that they didn't deserve Ilya? "We're going to be parents at last. It will make our relationship stronger. We shouldn't worry about how it's going to affect our sex life." Her voice dropped to a whisper as she added, "But I do. I feel like I'm already letting it affect our sex life because I'm so nervous about making everything perfect for him. And then I feel like a horrible selfish person for even thinking that." To her horror, her lips quivered as she fought back tears.

Immature. Selfish. Ilya had already been abandoned by one set of parents who weren't able to put his needs first. At least his birth parents might have had the excuse of being too young or too poor to take care of a baby. She had no such excuse. They were nearly forty, supposedly grown-ups with good jobs, though she was taking a long leave of absence and wasn't sure she'd end up going back. "Maybe I'm not ready for this," she confessed. "Maybe I never will be." Maybe their inability to conceive had been the universe's way of telling her that she wasn't cut out to be a mom, wasn't strong enough to make the necessary sacrifices.

"I think it's finally hitting you that cool as it is the adoption paperwork got fast-tracked, we're getting our kid in a few weeks instead of a few months like we'd thought and we're not as prepared as we'd hoped we'd be. Trust me, I already had my own freak-out. Hence the nice bottle of wine and the steaks...I figured we needed them."

For about the thousandth time in the turbulent adoption process, Stacy reflected that she'd picked a good man.

And a very sexy one, although that was probably not the best thing to think at the moment, not when she was so shaky, not when she wasn't sure if she wanted sex or a good cry or possibly both.

Tom hugged her close, gave her another kiss. She tried to feel only the tenderness in the kiss, the love, but she couldn't help it. The heat was there, too, and it sizzled into her. Her nipples crinkled and stood at attention. Her pussy twitched in anticipation. She pressed her breasts against Tom's chest, circling them a little to enjoy the slight stimulation.

Part of her felt like she should insist they get some work done on Ilya's room before they gave themselves license to play.

But the room would be there in the morning. They'd have plenty of time to paint and get the bright jungle-animal border up over the next couple of days.

Stacy's good intentions, Stacy's fears, Stacy's notions about how a mother should behave, were dissolving under Tom's kiss.

One of his hands cupped the back of her head, a subtle control that let her relax into the moment; into Tom's touch, Tom's body. The other hand pushed up her skirt. She was bare legged on this fine spring day, and her skirt was short. It wasn't long before Tom's hand was sliding inside the lacy hip band of her panties, sliding along the curve of her ass.

Stacy adjusted her stance, spreading her legs to encourage that questing hand. Soon it gripped hard, a possessive gesture that sent a guilty thrill through her.

She felt even guiltier when Tom gave her butt a light slap—not even a spank, more an exploratory tap to see how she'd respond—and she moaned and thrust her butt back in blatant invitation. She was a mom. Tom was a dad. Okay, their child wasn't living in the house yet, but they were Ilya's parents, or would be soon, as much so as if she was massively pregnant now and eagerly waiting for her due date. What kind of decent parents got into spanking games?

The kind of parents they would be, apparently. It shouldn't have surprised her, although on some level it did. They'd dabbled in kink, enjoying spanking and light bondage and occasional experiments with something more fierce. Why had she thought they'd suddenly become vanilla?

If the thrill, the very primal need, coursing through Stacy was any indication, they'd find a way to play sometimes, even if it was late at night and at the opposite side of the house from where Ilya was sleeping. They'd have to. She wondered how much of her recent tension was anxiety about the adoption and how much was horniness, the need for a good spanking and a hard fuck that they simply hadn't taken the time to indulge in lately.

"I've been thinking we have to be June and Ward squeaky-clean Cleaver to be good parents," she said seemingly out of nowhere, knowing that Tom would get it. "But Ilya will be better off if we're just us and happy."

"Duh," Tom said, not unkindly. "Though I suppose we'll have to keep the sex in the bedroom instead of wherever we get the urge." Then he spanked her again, harder this time, and before she could stop herself—before she could even remember why she thought she should stop herself—Stacy cried out, "Oh, god, I need that."

Tom whispered, "Take your panties off and lean on the counter."

The brand-new counter, the one they'd just finished installing last month.

Not that long ago, they'd have "broken in" the new counter right away, celebrating the renovation by seeing how many ways they could incorporate it into sex. With all they had going on, playing had slipped from the list of priorities, though, so it hadn't happened until now.

Stacy felt a flash of sorrow about that, followed by a much bigger flash of lustful glee that it was happening now. The damn guilt tried to work its way back into her consciousness, but she made herself ignore it. Their little boy wasn't even in the country yet, let alone wandering into the kitchen to wonder why Daddy was spanking Mommy. Definitely no reason to feel guilty.

Before her overdeveloped sense of responsibility made her change her mind, Stacy slithered out of her panties, gyrating more than necessary to give Tom a good show. She braced herself against the counter, stuck her ass out and wiggled it at Tom.

Tom gently, slowly, teasingly raised her skirt, making the simple gesture a ritual. The fabric slithered against Stacy's skin. She bit her lip to stifle a groan of need.

He ran his hand gently over her thrust-out ass. At that point, Stacy stopped trying to stifle her moans. The sound came out deep and throaty, shocking her with its raw, blatant desire. After feeling they shouldn't fool around, Stacy was now frantic for it, as if her efforts at self-control had only served to arouse her more. Her pussy throbbed, her thighs felt slick and damp, and Tom's featherlight touch was making her crazy. Forget that—the touch of the air was making her crazy. "Please," she begged, "Please," her voice hoarse with need.

Tom's hand came down hard on her ass. Pain and pleasure ricocheted through her body, jarring loose the guilt, the fear that she wouldn't be a good mother, that she'd be too wrapped up in Tom and neglect Ilya. She wasn't sure where the guilt and fear came from. At some point, now that she could see how absurd it was, she'd take the time to trace it back to its roots.

Right now, though, she was going to let the spanking carry her away. Right now, she was going to stop thinking and ride the delicious combination of pleasure and dull pain.

Each smack brought her closer to Tom, not the dad-to-be counterpart to her mom-to-be, but the lover she'd married and chosen to become a parent with, the whole package she adored including the kinks. The spanking and other minor fetishes were part of who they were together, a part of a love for each other so strong they knew they had to share it with a child who needed them. And they'd find a way to keep expressing their love for each other—their way—even while they made a safe and welcoming home for a child who'd never had one.

A particularly hard blow jarred her spine—jarred her heart, too, letting loose the last remnants of grief that another woman had carried their child, that she'd never give birth to a baby conceived in the fire of her love and passion for Tom. She hadn't realized she still harbored those regrets, thinking she'd replaced them with joy the first time Ilya smiled at them and said, in his laboring English, "I love you." But maybe it was natural for grief and joy to coexist, like pain and pleasure.

Tom spanked her several more times in rapid succession, too quick and hard for her to process immediately. It snapped her out of introspection and into orbit. Her drenched pussy gripped at nothing. She rode the rhythm of sharp shock transmuting to ecstasy, rode the waves of joy and panic triggered by Ilya's impending arrival, rode her love for Tom to a place where she laughed and cried and came all at once.

Crying, laughing, coming, she reached out for Tom and found he'd already unzipped his jeans. He slammed into her, his body slapping against her tender butt. At the same time, though, he kissed her neck and shoulder softly, sweetly.

Her pussy fluttered and squeezed at him, and she pushed back to meet his urgent thrusts. "Don't hold back," she whispered.

He didn't. It was a wildfire fuck, fast and urgent, each of them egging the other on until it almost hurt but instead was beautiful. At the end, as Tom came inside her and she exploded again along with him, Stacy swore she smelled something burning.

Then she realized she *did* smell burning. "The steaks!" she exclaimed, and Tom was laughing and cursing as he yanked his jeans up and hopped out the back door, still zipping up.

When Tom came back inside, he was shaking his head and still laughing. "The steaks are charcoal."

"I bet June Cleaver would never burn dinner because she was too busy fucking," Stacy mused out loud.

"Technically, *I* burned dinner, since I put the steaks on," Tom corrected her. "And I'm sure if Ward Cleaver forgot the steaks on the grill, he'd take June out for a nice dinner to apologize. How does sushi sound?"

"Perfect." She winked. "It's light enough that it won't weigh us down later. Quickies are good, but I imagine we'll be having a lot of those as parents. After dinner, I want to take our time."

THREE NIGHTS BEFORE THE WEDDING

Catherine Paulssen

She hated the sheer idea of it.

She hated the thought of having to feign enthusiasm over some sweaty Latin lover stripping on her lap. She hated that she was supposed to be thrilled to touch his slippery skin when all she could really think about was the warm, slightly dry skin of the man she loved. And she hated the drunken cows outside who had brought her into this situation.

The forced fun of bachelorette parties hadn't held any particular appeal for Imogene ever since the first leather-clad crotch had been shoved into her face at her cousin's party seven years ago.

Then, she had been appalled. Now, she was seething. And somewhat humiliated.

"Get off—damn it!" In another fit of fury at the mere thought of it, she rattled at the handcuffs that bound her to a stylish wall radiator, its horizontal pipes shimmering in tarnished gold against the dark crimson wall. She stomped her foot and cursed as she tried to no avail to wriggle her wrists out of the metal rings.

It must have been the stupidest idea she had ever heard. But her bachelorette bunch, consisting of two future sisters-in-law and their friends, had insisted.

Imogene sniffed a little. Her own girls would never have done this to her. But they were on the East Coast, and what could you do about your fiancé's kinfolks? She counted herself lucky that they at least had enough money to throw her a bachelorette party in a luxurious Las Vegas hotel.

After another apprehensive glance at the door, she took in the room. In one corner stood a plushy antique chair. The walls were adorned with gilt-framed pictures of 1920s vaudeville girls. From the corner of her eyes, she could spot part of a velveteen curtain that separated the room from a small vestibule.

It was a fancy room. A men's restroom, mind you, but fancy.

Still, the guys trying their luck in the hotel's casino weren't so different from the regular players in any low-grade arcade. A shudder ran down her spine at the thought of whatever drunken jerk might walk in on her, defenseless, abandoned by the party hosts, who were probably enjoying themselves at the blackjack table right now. The men that had been around while the girls had tied her up, cheering and laughing at her protests, weren't the kind of guys she had any desire of encountering again. She wondered how long it would take before they summoned all their wasted friends to have a feast gawking at the little lady chained up in their restroom, dressed in a cheap veil and a shirt that was so slinky her breasts looked ready for the centerfold. To complete her misery, she would have to persuade one of these boozed-up morons to pay her ransom. That was the deal.

For sure the stupidest idea that Michael's family had come up with in the preparations that would lead to their wedding next Saturday.

Imogene froze as the door was flung open and quick steps

rushed into the vestibule. A man in a hurry. She closed her eyes and drew a deep breath, wondering if she would have to listen to him peeing before she could ask him to pay whatever ransom he would be willing to spend on her. He entered the room, and she heard him exhale.

Well, she had to give it to him—it wasn't often that you found a sluttishly attired girl chained to the heater in the men's room.

"Excuse me, could you...um..."

He walked over to her, his steps slowing, and she bent her head, but her arms restricted her view of the entrance. She peeked down underneath the pit of her arm. The handcuffs bit into her wrists as she tried to turn, and yet the only glimpse she could catch of him were leather boots and the beginning of slender legs in black pants.

"Wow," he said, and his voice made her shudder. It reached something deep inside her and rolled through her veins, aiming directly at her core. "That must be the most wonderful thing I've seen all evening." His boots clicked on the marble floor as he stepped behind her and stopped at the basin stand next to the radiator. "And you can see a lot of pretty things on a night in Vegas," he added in a low, friendly voice.

"Surely not in a men's restroom," Imogene murmured, more to herself than to him. He chuckled a bit.

"Surely not."

She decided to cut right to the chase. "I need someone to ransom me."

"Have you been naughty to deserve this?"

She held her breath. "Are you flirting with me?"

"Maybe."

She heard the rustling of jeans and saw him crossing his feet. She could practically feel his eyes all over her body. His scent was warm and smelled of fresh soap and cardamom. Imogene exhaled. "Don't you think that would be taking advantage of my situation?"

"Maybe."

"Would you pay my ransom if I flirted back?"

"Maybe."

Imogene rested her head against her arm. "Sounds fair."

He circled around and leaned against the wall in front of her. "That's what I think. But even if you didn't consider it fair, the way I see it, you're not in much of a bargaining position."

"That's not a very gentleman-like thing to say."

"I'm not a gentleman then. How fitting that your shirt is too tight to belong to a lady."

She rolled her eyes. "Tell me something I don't know."

He laughed, abandoning the smoldering tone that had thickened his voice until now. "You're pretty cheeky for someone tied to a radiator."

"There must be something about you that makes me trust you."

The guy whistled. "I see. But what would your future husband say?" He threw a quick glance at the short pink veil attached to the rhinestone tiara in her hazel hair.

She matched the look in his dark eyes as they turned to her face again. "He wants to see me walking down the aisle in three days, so I guess he wouldn't mind."

He tilted his head and puckered his lips into the hint of a smile. "With all due respect to the lucky guy, he's not taking good care of you."

She raised her eyebrows. "You think?"

"Uh-huh." He reached out his finger and traced it down the line of her arm. Imogene held her breath as her eyes followed the trail of his tease. "If I were him, I'd make sure you'd be tied to"—he ran his long finger up her arm again and, in a playful gesture, moved it over the metal ring and drew a circle in her palm—"nothing but my bedpost."

She bit her lip. "He never does things like that."

"Maybe it's time for him to experiment."

Her heart skipped a beat. "Maybe."

Imogene watched him expectantly, the sparkles that glimmered in his stare making the blood rush to her cheeks. She lowered her gaze to his mouth and licked her lips. "Come here, baby," she purred, smiling at him as he obeyed, his face lighting up. He slowly wrapped his arms around her. "Thank you," she breathed before they melted into each other.

"Thank you for what?" he whispered as their lips parted.

"For being my hero and coming to my rescue!" She threw an annoyed glance at the handcuffs binding her.

"I'm sorry. I'm sorry for my crazy family. You didn't cry, did you?" Michael brushed his thumb over a smear of mascara on her cheek.

"A little bit, maybe." She pouted and lowered her head.

He lifted her chin with his thumb and pulled her a bit closer to him. "I'm here now." He placed another small kiss on her lips. Imogene pressed her body against his. Unable to hug him, she wanted to at least show him how thankful she was. His handsome features had been the last she expected to see tonight, and to be bathed in that tender glow of his dark eyes, a shimmer that had been deepened since his proposal six months ago, turned her giddy inside.

"How did you find me?"

"Martin blabbed. He said something about ransom, so I pressured him to tell me where they had gone with you and what games they had made up."

She rubbed her leg against his. "I'm so glad you did."

"I know how much you loathe pranks."

"This one took a surprisingly nice turn."

Michael returned her smile and ran his hands over her curves. "So you'd like me to experiment, huh?" he said softly against her mouth, teasing her by gently prodding her lips.

"You came here especially for me. You can do anything you want."

"Anything?"

"Yes…" she breathed against his lips.

His hand brushed along her waistline. "You know that rule you came up with a couple of weeks ago?"

"No sex before getting married?"

"Uh-huh." He parted her hair and placed a kiss on her neck. "I never liked it in the first place."

"I just wanted…" Imogene craned her neck. "I wanted us to feel like…they did in the old days."

"But we already slept together anyways." Michael grinned at her. "With everything we did, you should be ashamed to even *think* about walking down the aisle in virgin white."

She shook her head, smiling a little, amused by the impatience in his voice. "You don't get it, huh?"

"No, as a matter of fact, I don't." He imbibed the smell of her hair and softly blew against her skin. "What's the point of being with the most beautiful girl in the world when you don't get to make love to her?"

Tiny butterflies fluttered through her stomach, and for a moment, she simply enjoyed the freshly fallen-in-love feeling he could evoke in her, even after two years of being together. "I figured it would be a thrill. You know, increasing the anticipation."

He smiled and kissed his way up to her ear. "It did."

"So you do get it after all." She sighed and closed her eyes.

"You still want to wait?" he teased her, softly biting her ear's outer shell.

"No," she whispered, turning her head to kiss him.

"Good," he simply replied and circled her belly button with his thumb.

"But what if...what if someone walks in on us?"

Michael pulled away a bit, and the expression on his face changed. "I'll be back."

Before she could protest, he had stormed out of the room. Moments later, she heard him lock the door. "Everything's settled," he grinned, slightly out of breath.

"How did you—?"

"Shhh." He scooped her up in his arms again and kissed her. For a few moments, he entertained himself with making her try to catch his lips in vain, backing away every time she came close enough before finally sealing her raspberry-colored mouth with a kiss. Imogene could feel his cock swelling against her as his fingers wandered down her hips and found the space between the top of her jeans skirt and the bottom of her shirt where her skin was exposed.

"You're beautiful," he whispered and traced her navel.

She pulled a face. "The shirt's tacky, and I feel stupid wearing it."

"But you *are* property of the groom," he said, referring to the phrase printed over her chest in iridescent colors. Mischief glinting in the corner of his eyes, he leaned back a bit to read it all. "Now and forever." He nipped her with his hands clasped around her waist. "I don't see what's wrong with that. The girls got it damn right!"

She rolled her eyes at him and turned around as far as she could.

"Buy me a shot, I'm tying the knot." Michael laughed. "Want me to strip it off?"

Imogene's eyes flashed below her lashes and she bit her

bottom lip, her eyes turning to his mouth.

"Do you?" His hands rubbed her back underneath the shirt. She licked her lips. "Yes."

"Yes?" he breathed, his eyes watching her as his face moved closer to hers.

"Yes, baby," she moaned softly before meeting his lips. Michael let the tip of his tongue dance with hers for a few tantalizing flutters, then took a step back. With one swift movement, he grabbed the shirt's end and ripped it apart, right through the printing in the middle. She wiggled her upper body in his arms and captured his lips again. "Get it off!"

Michael tore apart the sleeves and stripped the shreds off of her. She purred, satisfied, and wrapped one leg around him. He buried his face between her breasts, playfully tugging at the strapless red bra with his teeth. She threw back her head as they skimmed her nipples, but stiffened the next moment when she heard someone at the door. Eyes widened with shock, she pressed her body against him.

"Don't worry," he whispered, softly sucking at her skin. "It's just the barman."

"The barman?"

He grinned and reached into the pocket of his jacket. "I *persuaded* him to put an out-of-order sign on the door." Slowly, he produced a key and let it run down, between her breasts to her navel. She sighed as the cool metal brushed her skin. "And the only other key is with the janitor…"

"What about a key for these?" She rattled the handcuffs.

He kissed her neck. "I didn't bother searching for any familiar-looking chicks in pink shirts."

She gyrated her hips against his crotch. "That gives you a nice pretense to experiment…"

Michael uttered a muffled affirmation while opening her

skirt's button, then bent down to slide it off her legs. His eyes sparkled as they detected the dark red mesh panties underneath. "Did you...?" he gasped. He tugged at them to confirm what he thought he'd discovered below the see-through textile. "You got so much more than just a manicure the other day!" he exclaimed.

Imogene ducked her head. "I wanted to surprise you on our wedding night. It's called *The Heart*. You like it?" She let out a little squeak as his forefinger traced the new shape of her bush, deliberately brushing her moist pussy while exploring.

He got on his knees and pulled down her panties. "Very much," he muttered, kissing the heart's lines. "It's extremely sexy."

"As is your head down there," she moaned softly.

"I can't believe you did that." His tongue darted at her bare skin. "Did it hurt?"

She leaned against the wall and closed her eyes. "Only a little...a little bit," she panted.

He brushed her clit with his thumb while the caress of his mouth turned to her navel. "I'll make up for that."

Imogene spread her legs as far as she could with her arms bound to the radiator. The pressure of his thumb circling her clit increased, but she couldn't give the sensations her full attention. "Michael?"

"Hmm?" He looked up.

"I had so many scenarios in mind of how I would reveal this to you." She giggled.

Michael got up and grinned at her. He kissed her lips, then lifted her up. "Wrap your legs around me. Come on." He grabbed her thighs and pulled her close. His hardened cock pressed against her; Imogene sighed as he ground it against her clit, which was now exposed to the rough material of his jeans.

She arched her back a bit to increase the friction. Michael fixed his eyes on her erect nipples, perked up so close to his face that every brush of his breath against them sent a trace of goose bumps over her breasts. He gave in to their charms and enclosed the left one with his lips. Imogene threw back her head as he softly sucked on it. The more his tongue probed, the more she became aware of how powerless she was. With a frustrated groan, she yanked at the cuffs. Michael interrupted the caress of his mouth and smirked. He let go of her thighs and moved his hands up to her wrists and from there, down to the pit of her arms. His light touch tickled her, but before she could plead for him to stop, he put an end to this taunting. Her eyes followed the trail of his fingers as it reached her breasts, and the realization that she was in for an even more intense tease sent a shudder down her spine. As if indecisive about what to do, Michael circled the same nipple with his finger that he had just spoiled with his mouth.

"You like being cuffed." He watched her face for any reaction.

Imogene licked her dry lips. She closed her eyes and let herself fall into the sensations. His huge hands cupped her breasts. His breath stroked her naked skin. She wanted nothing more than to roam his body with her hands. A tiny flame licked at her clit, and the urgent pulsation raging between her legs every time he withheld a caress betrayed how much the fact of being bound sparked a desire she hadn't been aware of before. She knew she would let him tie her up again anytime he wanted.

"I do," she heard herself saying.

"Mm-hmm." He licked away a bead of sweat that had formed between her breasts. He cupped her butt and pressed her against the radiator. One of his hands wandered between her legs. He started to stroke her wet pussy with two fingers. "I can tell."

Again, she rattled at the handcuffs—a reflex driven by the urge to wrap herself around him completely, press her body so close to his that she could taste his skin, smell his warmth. Desperation rushed through her, a heated, frantic desperation that dissolved into sizzling tingles exploding under the surface of her skin.

Michael kissed the underside of her breast, and she held her breath as his lips wandered up to her right nipple, then stopped, tantalizingly close. They almost touched her; she could feel the heat of them against her skin. And yet, he wouldn't appease her yearning, and with every push she made, he backed his mouth away until the metal rings restrained her from moving any farther. Excruciatingly slowly, the tip of his tongue became visible, at first only to lick his own lip. Her eyes pleaded with him, and she quivered when his mouth finally met her swollen nipple and engulfed it tenderly.

"Take off your pants," she breathed against his lips. "I don't want to wait any longer."

Michael moaned. "Say that again."

"I want to have you." She nibbled at his lip. "Inside of me. Now."

He let her down again and got rid of his clothes. Imogene gnawed at her bottom lip as his hardened cock emerged. Everything within her wanted to get her hands on it and spread the thin drop that dripped off the top generously across the glistening head. Michael met her stare with hardened, aroused eyes. He grabbed her naked butt and yanked her against him.

Her eyes rolled to the back of her head as his cock filled her and was slowly withdrawn again. He knew how to make her burn, even now. Just one look into his agitated face and the relieved moan he formed in his throat when her walls clenched his cock told her he was simmering just as much as she was.

Imogene writhed against the handcuffs, fiercely channeling all her force into her thighs to unleash the overwhelming ecstasy. Instead of her hands, it was her feet that dug into his flesh, almost kicking his butt to make him push harder.

His thrusts intensified, but she could tell he was holding back. Her fingers clutched one of the radiator's pipes, and she rocked her hips into his strokes.

A short smile flickered over Michael's face. "Don't be that impatient. You waited long enough for this orgasm."

She shook her head. "Don't you dare tease me, Michael. Don't you—" She gulped as he pulled his length away. It glistened with her cream. He splayed her legs even farther, enclosed his shaft in his hands and circled her throbbing clit with it. All she could do was watch and whimper.

"Please…" She lifted her head, searching for his mouth. He briefly brushed her open lips, his tongue teasing her longer than his mouth kissed her, his breath heavy on her face. As slowly as he had taken it away from her, he plunged his cock inside her again. His fingers curled around hers as he started to rock her, making her forget about the painful rubbing of the handcuffs against her wrists.

"Oh, baby, that's—" She didn't finish her sentence, for at that moment, fists banged against the door and she heard her name yelled by upset female voices. "*Now?* You're worried *now?*"

Michael groaned while the noises at the door got louder. "Let them dangle."

"Imogene, are you in there?"

"Oh, Michael, don't stop," she moaned into his mouth. "Don't stop now…"

"Please answer! Sweetie, we're—"

"She's coming," Michael yelled. He ran the back of his fingers along her temple. "She's coming," he said softly and intensified his thrusts. "She's coming," he panted as he pushed her to heights that made her forget about the world outside. Heat shot behind Imogene's navel and from there, spread through her body, blanketing her in blissful exhaustion.

With a sigh, she eased her body into his, and he held her tight for some minutes after they came down. The banging at the door had stopped, and she enjoyed his kisses on her neck and the assurance of his love whispered into her ear.

"I want to hug you! And I think I can't feel my hands anymore," she added, only half joking.

Michael looked around, a bit at a loss. "Wait, maybe…" He kissed her hair and let go of her, causing her to shiver as the warmth of his body was taken away from her. "Let's try this," he murmured and applied soap from the dispenser to her wrists, then rubbed the handcuffs against them. "Does it hurt?"

She shook her head. "I barely feel them, really."

Michael regarded the reddened skin with concern. "I'm going to pull a bit harder once, okay? You need to tell me if it hurts too much."

She nodded and bit her teeth.

"Now!" It did hurt. Even through the numbness of her arms, she could feel the pain stinging her.

At last, Michael got her hands out of both metal rings. "You're free," he smiled and took her hands in his. "Poor baby." He inspected the blotchy skin. "Come here."

A rush of tenderness surged through her as she watched him rinsing her wrists in cool water. "I love you so much."

He just smiled then carefully dried her hands and arms. He reached for the bottle of lotion next to the sink and massaged the soothing cream into her swollen skin.

"I wonder what they'd have said if you had asked them for the key a few minutes ago," Imogene giggled.

Michael's smile became wider. He lowered his gaze to her irritated skin and softly brushed it with his thumbs. "Would you rather have the wedding without them?"

She slid her arms around his neck. "How would we do that?"

He gave her a peck on her mouth. "We'd skip the big party."

Her eyes widened as she understood his idea. "Well, I do have the veil," she grinned.

Michael threw an amused glance at the pink piece of tulle. "You sure do."

She looked at him, intrigued, but wanted a moment to consider his proposal. "Let's sit down here for a while, hmm?"

He placed his jacket on the floor for her to sit on, then handed her his black long-sleeved shirt. "Here, put that on."

She buried her nose in the fabric and sighed with pleasure. "This is one shirt I love to wear."

Michael leaned in for a kiss and laced his fingers through hers. "What do you want?"

She smiled lovingly at him. "What can I choose from?"

"Late summer breeze or early autumn rain."

"Early autumn rain."

He gave her a tender glance, then bent over her hand and covered it with small, quick kisses, followed by a soft tickling with the fingers of his other hand.

"Now do the summer breeze."

Michael led her hand to his lips and kissed it, his lips in a pout, his tongue darting at it. He blew on the skin that his mouth had caressed and ended his treat with a tender kiss on her fingers. She gently squeezed his hand. "When you first played that with me, the night after Martin's party, I knew you were the guy I wanted to marry. I knew that if you ever asked me, I'd say yes without hesitation."

"I meant what I said." He was serious now. "You just say the word, and I'll marry you right now in some gaudy chapel across the strip."

"You wouldn't miss your family? And all our friends?"

Michael shrugged. "We can still celebrate with them later."

She held his gaze. Her heart already knew the answer, but her head tried to figure out if there was any reason that spoke against it. "I do," she whispered eventually.

Michael's face lit up. He kissed her hand then jumped up, helping her onto her feet. "Do you want me to buy you anything? Something new?"

"I think I'm all good. I even have something borrowed, something blue..." She tugged at the shirt and looked down at her skirt. "But I'd like to have a wedding bouquet."

"Of course." He cupped her face with his hands, kissed her tenderly and adjusted the tiara. "My beautiful bride."

An hour later, Mendelssohn's "Wedding March" filled a small sugary chapel next to the MGM Grand. Imogene's gaze took in Michael, beaming at her from an altar covered in garlands of plastic lilies, then she looked down at her own appearance. She hid a bashful smile in the exquisite bouquet of white roses he had given her and shook her head a little. A sparkling chandelier was dimmed above her head, and she thought about how much this getup differed from the plans they had made for their big reception. The groom was dressed in jeans and a white V-neck shirt; the bride wore a black long-sleeve that almost covered the whole of her miniskirt. Their only guest was a photographer whose service came as part of the wedding package.

But as Elvis walked her down the aisle and she locked eyes with the man her heart loved with every beat and every fiber, the butterflies in her stomach told her for certain that this bachelor-ette party was the best she had ever attended.

FLOWERING

Donna George Storey

I'm supposed to be reading an article for my teaching seminar. Instead I'm watching Daniel.

More specifically, I'm watching Daniel weed his garden. It's a surprisingly compelling way to spend a Saturday afternoon. Daniel has his back to me, which means I get a great view of his jeans hugging his muscular ass as he bends and straightens then pauses, weight resting jauntily on one leg, to survey his progress. Sometimes he turns slightly toward me, and I can feast my eyes on his large hands as they yank away the messy tangles of green to reveal nude brown earth.

I shift on the armchair, aware of the subtle throbbing between my legs. I've learned a lot about my landlord from watching him this past month. Even more than I learned the night we had sex, exactly four weeks ago. I know he appears at the kitchen window around seven-thirty each weekday morning to make himself some kind of smoothie in a blender. On Monday evenings after he gets back from work, he often watches football on the big TV in his family room, his feet propped on the coffee table, a beer in his hand. I've counted three friends who stop by regularly—two equally athletic men also in their late twenties and a slightly older, very voluptuous woman, who crushes him to her breasts for hellos and good-byes, but otherwise doesn't touch him like a lover. I know where his bedroom is, too, on the right-hand corner of the second floor of his handsome California Craftsman. Usually the drawn shade glows gold until close to midnight, but the few times he's left it open, I could just make out a shadowy figure moving in the dim room, as restless as my memory.

Suddenly Daniel pivots and glances toward the cottage. I jump guiltily then drop my eyes to the course reader in my lap. It's unlikely he can see me since my armchair is placed well back from the window. Even if he can, he's probably not the least interested in what I'm doing. Men are much better at compartmentalizing and moving on.

In spite of this unforeseen complication—that I'm both lusting after and doing my best to avoid further personal contact with my attractive neighbor—I'm still lucky to have scored one of the most charming one-bedroom rentals in Berkeley for under a thousand bucks a month. My cousin got her law degree at Boalt a few years ago, and I had the insider friend-of-a-friend track. Ironically, one of the reasons I chose to get my master's in teaching on the West Coast, when there were plenty of perfectly good programs in New York, was to extricate myself from a complicated romantic relationship.

And all I did was run right back into a tangle.

I suspect neither of us saw what was coming when Daniel suggested we have dinner at Cesar's tapas bar by way of introducing me to the neighborhood. He was friendly but reserved as we shared garlic fries and seared sea scallops and duck tacos. He did mention, before the mojitos arrived, that his mother had passed away six months before following a long battle with cancer. That was why he'd assumed the premature role of owner of some prime East Bay real estate.

"It was lucky for me Janice could introduce me to someone responsible to rent the cottage. It saved me a lot of hassle."

All I could manage in reply was a sympathetic humming sound, which probably seemed insensitive. The truth was, I knew plenty about illnesses and funerals and the numb days that follow. I didn't want to put a damper on our pleasant dinner, though, so I took the cheerful route.

"I'm the lucky one. I fell in love with the place the moment I saw it. And I love the furnishings, too. Very Berkeley."

He smiled and told me that he'd made the kitchen table and chairs himself. He liked to do things with his hands. I couldn't help casting a glance at those capable hands now resting just a few inches from mine. And I fell in love with him a little bit more.

I shouldn't have had the third mojito. I probably shouldn't have had the second either, but I didn't want the evening to end. Daniel and I were hitting it off, and by the time we staggered back home, we were laughing like old friends. As I fumbled with the latch of the gate back to the garden, Daniel raised an eyebrow.

"Come on, you need some coffee," he said, steering me into the "big house" as I'd already begun to call it. His hands felt lusciously warm and strong on my shoulders. It wasn't really sex that I was after at that point, but the thought of going back to my cottage alone made my skin ache with a nameless sorrow.

I started wanting sex in the worst way, however, as I watched him make the coffee. Grinding the beans, tipping the loamy powder into the French press, pouring out the water while he bit his lip adorably. Our hands touched when he handed me the mug. Delicious as the brew smelled, I never even took a sip, because he leaned forward and kissed me then, tentatively, his soft lips offset by the roughness of his five o'clock shadow. I put the mug on the counter and slipped my hands around his waist. My mouth was slightly numb from the tequila, but Daniel's lips had a strange magic, sinking deeper into me, to a place where I could feel every sensation exquisitely.

Farther down I could feel his erection rising in his jeans—and an answering flutter of desire between my legs. A moan leaked from my lips as I pressed my body shamelessly against him. I wanted to burrow into him, so hot and hard and soft all at the same time.

Daniel pulled away. "Are you sure, Elizabeth? I know you're a little drunk."

"I want to do this," I insisted. And in that tiny corner of my brain that is always sober, I wanted to do this very, very much.

"I want to, too," he whispered.

And so he led me upstairs to another bedroom, opposite to the one I'd seen illuminated at night. The silver glow of the full moon revealed a sleigh bed of dark wood, a snow-white bedspread, a pretty Japanese bowl on the nightstand. Even in my tipsy haze, I understood it was a guest room, probably little used even when his mother was alive. Desperate to banish the museum-like stillness, I immediately pulled him down on top of me, and we kissed again, devouring each other like dessert.

I still squirm when I remember that night. Daniel took great delight in the responsiveness of my breasts, murmuring how beautiful I was as he kissed and suckled my diamond-hard nipples. Once he had me gasping and twisting beneath him, he slid down between my legs, peeling away my jeans and panties with eager hands. At first he kissed my vulva patiently, even politely, until my lips swelled and my clit throbbed and I was whimpering and juicing all over the bed. When he finally snaked his pointy tongue between my folds to my sweet spot, I groaned and clutched his shoulders as if he'd just saved my life. With a groan himself, he pushed my feet up and back, spreading me wide, then touched his mouth to me and began to hum.

"Oh, fuck, oh, fuck, oh, fuck me," I moaned.

"I want you to come on my face." His soft voice had a surprising authority.

It would have been exactly the right trick a few years before, but I'd brought another desire to this bed. My previous lover, an older man fresh from a divorce, had patiently taught me to have orgasms during intercourse, which is probably why I stayed with him far longer than I should have. Now I wanted to know if I could do it without him.

"Please, I want your cock inside."

Daniel smiled, his lips and chin glistening with my wetness. "I'll be right back."

And he was, condom in hand.

"Come on, climb on top." His nonchalance made me wonder how many women he'd taken on this bed, but even that idea, that I was his one-off slut of the weekend, excited me. He certainly knew how to please a woman. Because of course, when I was perched on his cock, he could easily slip a finger between us to rub my swollen clit. I writhed and rode him until I didn't need his finger anymore. It was enough to grind myself against him while he pinched and sucked my nipples. I bellowed like an animal when I climaxed—god, yes, it *was* possible to do this without Frank—and Daniel took his turn, grabbing my ass and thrusting up into me with surprising ferocity. He came with staccato barks that, it struck me later, sounded very much like sobs.

I collapsed onto him and gave the pillow a secret smile.

"Wow," he said. Then again, "Wow."

"Aren't you glad I threw myself at you?" I murmured in his ear.

"Am I ever." He laughed. "Do you want to stay over here tonight? I'd like that."

Once again, he'd done just the right thing. How could I refuse?

We curled up in each other's arms, our bodies fitting easily together. My last waking thought was how strange it was that such a sweet-faced man was so hot in bed from the first kiss all the way through the afterglow.

I woke with a shudder, as if someone had smacked the bed with a huge hand. It was still dark outside. The windows rattled and the walls groaned. Was this a famous California earthquake?

Daniel was sleeping at the far edge of the bed with his back to me, undisturbed by the tremor.

I lay quietly on my side of the bed, feeling scared and alone. It didn't seem right to wake him and ask for comfort. We were nothing more than strangers after all. He might as well have picked me up at the bar. Suddenly it was unbearable to keep pretending I had a reason to be there. I quickly dressed and let myself out the back door. Back in my cottage, I jumped into the shower and scrubbed myself vigorously as if I could somehow make it all like it was before, with nothing more between us than a glimmer of attraction that would never be fulfilled.

Why was it always the fulfilled fantasies that got me into trouble?

I didn't see Daniel at all the next day. I assumed he was avoiding me as much as I was him. Two days later our paths did cross as I was returning from my evening seminar and he was coming back from a run. I noted, with a pang, that he looked good in shorts.

"Lindsey," he called out with such determination, I had to stop. He seemed about to say something more, but then his lips lifted in a polite smile. "Friends and good neighbors, okay?" He held out his hand.

I shook it. I can still feel that smooth palm in mine.

Daniel is moving toward me, a pair of clippers in his hand. He squats and starts attacking the withered ivy along the path to my cottage.

Again I feel that poignant twisting in my chest, as if something trapped inside is trying to break free. Daniel called me "responsible" that night at the tapas bar, and here I am acting like an obsessed teenager. That's when I resolve to do what I should have done a month ago. Live up to my grown-up's pledge. *Friends and good neighbors.*

I toss the course reader onto the end table and march to my door before I have a chance to change my mind.

Daniel looks up at me. His eyes flicker, then grow cautious.

"Hey," I manage to croak out.

"Hey, Lindsey, what's up?"

"Would you like some help? This looks like a big job."

His face softens. He hesitates, then says, "Sure. That would be great. I'll be right back."

A perverse part of me wants to laugh, remembering that's exactly what he said before he fetched the condom, but of course instead he hands over some gardening gloves and a sharp trowel with instructions to dig up the remaining roots and stems.

"How are classes going?" he asks when we've both found our working rhythm.

This is exactly what I hoped would happen. Good neighbors

make small talk. They don't spy and dream of sweet, sweaty couplings that will never happen again.

Soon we're chatting with ease. He tells me about the plans for the new landscaping, designed by a friend's wife: a Zen rock garden with a stone lantern surrounded by plants and shrubs that will flower in each season, a cherry for spring, a maple for autumn, rosemary for winter and Mexican sages for the dry summer months.

"When I was growing up we always had a vegetable garden in the backyard in the summer," I say, panting slightly from the digging and pulling. "Fresh peas and beans and corn and squash. I remember the zucchini terrified me. They could grow the size of a baseball bat after a good August storm."

Daniel laughs. "It never rains in August here, so we'd keep the zucchini in line. When you mentioned you were from New York, I assumed the city, but I guess your parents have some space to grow things. Do they still have a garden?"

I pause. Does he need my sad story to add to his own? And yet, I've wanted him to know we have something important in common since our ill-fated dinner.

I clear my throat. "My parents both passed away, my father when I was in high school, my mother a few years ago." My voice catches as I speak, but afterward I feel oddly light and cool, as if someone has opened a door and let the breeze in.

He is silent for a moment. "I'm sorry to hear that."

I continue digging at a stubborn root.

"You were so young to lose both parents. That must have been hard."

"I have an older sister. We look out for each other."

"I have an older sister, too. She lives in Chicago. And my dad's in L.A. My parents divorced when I was in high school. We keep in touch though."

I glance over at him. Our eyes meet. Suddenly I feel more naked than I ever did in bed with him, but his gaze holds mine just long enough to reassure me. *I understand.*

Working together, we clear away all the weeds and ivy beside my cottage in no time at all.

As dusk falls, Daniel offers to get a pizza for dinner to pay me back for all my help. I say yes, casually, as a friend and neighbor would surely do. Daniel has handed me a second chance. And this time I'll do it right.

A few hours later, I'm in his kitchen, showered and dressed in my casual best, finishing up my second slice of pizza from the Cheeseboard. Rich with feta and corn and fresh basil, the food is almost as intoxicating as a mojito. However, I made sure to turn down the beer he offered with dinner, noting that he placed the chilled bottle back in the refrigerator and poured us both water instead. So far so good with my plan to transform a hasty hookup into a real friendship.

I try to do the dishes, but Daniel graciously refuses. So again I find myself watching him at work and enjoying the view more than I'd like to admit. Who wouldn't be mesmerized by those thick, soapy fingers rubbing the dripping sponge round and round on the slick white plates? I relax back against the counter by the sink, then immediately jerk myself upright. I've unwittingly moved to the exact spot where we first kissed—and I'm determined that tonight, nothing will be like the last time.

Daniel looks at me quizzically. Then he smiles. "Oh, yes, I'm thinking of putting a plaque there."

"I'm sorry?"

"That's the Place Where It All Began That Night. Don't you remember?" His grin widens.

"Actually I assumed *you'd* forgotten," I blurt out.

He lifted his eyebrows at me as if it was unthinkable. In spite of myself, I laugh.

"Now," he continues, wiping his wet hands on a towel by the sink. "I hope you're not too full, because I also bought dessert for us. They're called 'adult brownies,' but I know you're of legal age."

"What does 'adult' mean for a brownie? That it's eighteen years old?"

We're both laughing now, even without the benefit of tequila.

"Let's taste it and find out." Daniel breaks off a chunk of the sturdy brownie and holds it out to me. My stomach does a flip. I'll have to touch his hand to take it. But friends do things like this all the time without a thought. I pluck it quickly from his palm.

"It's good," I murmur. "More dark chocolate than sugar. That must be why it's 'adult.'"

"The chocolate is pretty intense," he agrees. "More?"

"Yes, please."

This time he holds it out to my lips. His eyes twinkle.

In spite of myself I lean forward and take both the brownie and his fingertips between my lips.

The thing about sex is that sometimes you can't quite be sure how you get from one step to the next. How is it then that Daniel and I, the pair of us wounded and wary, are suddenly smashing our faces together in a desperate, chocolate-flavored kiss? This time his skin is silky smooth and moist—he must have shaved especially for me—and he is the one who moans and takes my face in both hands, as if to claim me.

He pulls away just far enough to whisper, "Are you sure?"

My reply is to slip my tongue into his mouth.

Somehow we get up the stairs, stopping to kiss deeply every

few steps. Daniel leads me to the same bedroom, which is as perfectly neat as if it hadn't been disturbed in years. But once we're naked under the cool sheets, our bodies twine together, as if we'd never been apart these long, lonely weeks. To think just a short time ago I could only watch. Now my senses are full of him. I'm tasting his sweet lips and touching his hot flesh and savoring his intimate male scent.

Daniel seems just as hungry as I am, moaning as he lavishes kisses on my neck and shoulders and breasts. I wonder if he's doing things to me that he's dreamed of for four long weeks, too. Suddenly he rolls on top of me, his strong thighs trapping my legs, pinning me in place. Taking my nipple between his lips, he plays it skillfully with his tongue. Then his hand slides up my neck, grabs a fistful of hair and pulls my head gently but firmly back into the pillow. A jolt of desire shoots down to my pussy. I've never felt so utterly possessed and enveloped.

He teases me until I'm so crazy with lust, I beg him to make love to me.

"Once you have your way with me, how do I know that you won't run away again?" It's that low, smoky sex voice I love, teasing but perfectly assured.

I whimper and shake my head.

But he still holds me fast with his body as he reaches for the nightstand drawer and pulls out a condom. As dazed as I am, I have to smile. He's wanted this, too, even planned for it. Kneeling above me, he quickly sheathes himself, then slips one leg between mine and spreads my legs. With one motion, he pushes his cock in so deep, I can feel his balls wedged into the crack of my ass.

"I want *you* to fuck *me*," he whispers, and after a moment of confusion, I sense what he's asking. I begin to move, pushing my hips up against his strong stomach. Each thrust brings a little bonus, the sweet friction of his sac sliding along my tender back furrow. All the while he suckles my nipples, which are enjoying this reunion with his lips very much. The pleasure builds in my body, a pulsing core of heat between my legs, until I can bear it no longer. I explode with a cry, my pussy milking him helplessly. Daniel takes the cue, pounding into me faster and harder until he cries out and shudders in my arms.

And only then do I admit to myself that this is what I *really* wanted all along.

Daniel strokes my hair as we lie together on the moon-drenched bed, letting the sweat cool. "How could you think I'd forget you?"

I laugh. "Not 'forget' exactly. But a stud like you probably has women throwing themselves at him all the time."

"Are you kidding? Being with you is the only good thing that's happened to me since…"

His words trail off, but he doesn't need to finish. I should have known from the sheer intensity, the touch of sadness in his pleasure, that he was seeking solace as much as sex.

I give his arm a squeeze. *I understand.*

"Why did you leave that night, Lindsey? Did I do something wrong?" There's no accusation in his voice. It's a genuine question.

Another joke flits through my head—*I didn't exactly leave if I'm still living in your backyard, right?*—but Daniel deserves better. I take a deep breath. "Maybe it's that you did everything right. It's scary to care for someone. If you care, you might lose them."

"True enough," he murmurs.

"Were you mad at me?"

"Not really mad, just confused," he says, pulling me closer.

"Actually you helped me see something that night. I had been thinking I might sell this place. Financially, it makes sense to keep it, but I'm still camping out in my old room. A single bed, soccer trophies, books from high school. I felt trapped in the past here. And then you...we...well, I realized I could make this my place own. I just have to start living in it and making my own memories."

"We've made a few memories on this mattress."

"Most definitely."

We laugh.

"Lindsey?"

"Hmm?"

"I have a favor to ask. Feel free to say no. Would you help me put in the garden? We can start with fall plantings now, then do more in the spring. Maybe put in a vegetable garden?"

I feel a tugging in my chest, as if a tight knot is easing itself loose.

"I'd like that a lot. And I have a favor to ask you, too."

"Don't plant any zucchini?"

"Well, maybe, but...I'd like to stay here tonight, really stay, if that's okay with you?"

His reply is simply to laugh, low and deep. Then his hand clasps mine, just like a handshake—friends and good neighbors—but this time there's new magic in his fingers. Because when I close my eyes, I don't see darkness. Instead I see floating before me the garden and its fresh expanse of bare brown earth from which, I know for certain, something beautiful will grow.

TEACH ME

Jeanette Grey

He isn't very good at this.

He's an athlete, Lissa thinks. All lean muscles and long limbs. Fingers that don't quite reach his toes when he forward-folds. As she presses back to downward dog, she keeps her gaze on him, itching to correct his form. *Hips to arms in one straight line, heels reaching for the floor.* He fumbles on without her intervention, looking awkward and maybe, possibly, pained.

The instructor cues them from the front. "Two deep breaths here."

Lissa lets the air fill her lungs, then pushes it back out. Once. Twice. But she can't quite find her focus.

It's unsettling. Strange, to be so distracted.

"Lift into three-point."

In a move her muscles know by heart, she sweeps her leg to the sky then swings it forward, plants her foot between her hands and rises. It's just a basic lunge, but the change in altitude still makes her breath quicken and her pulse pound. She savors the feeling, aches to fall into it, but out of the corner of her eye, she catches movement where there should only be stillness.

To her side, he wavers, teeters before finding his balance. In this pose, his legs look even longer, the smooth cording of his shoulders clear as his arms lift high. Lissa frowns. His chest isn't open, and his knee is too far forward. She glances to the teacher, who's already moving on, oblivious to the errors in form.

"Bring your hands to prayer and twist."

She turns toward him as he turns away.

He's beautiful, really, even if he's not much of a yogi. His hair is dark with sweat, his skin an inviting gold. In any other setting, he'd be graceful, too. She'd bet anything he would.

"Back to center."

Her gaze lingers just a second too long, her torso still twisting as he straightens, and his eyes meet hers. They're a deep brown, wide and warm. There's something honest to them, she thinks. Something made all the more attractive when, out of nowhere, he smiles.

She comes out of the pose with a start, blushing as she joins the rest of the class in forward fold. With her legs straight, she bends at the waist and lets her torso dangle, lets the blood rush to her face. When they rise to standing again, she chances a glance at him to find him glancing at her, too.

She has to force herself to look away.

For the next few poses, she keeps her gaze focused straight ahead, but eventually it's too much temptation. She seeks him out in the mirror, peering past the other twisting bodies to see just his face—just his eyes, the deep brown of his irises as they focus on her.

Conscious of the weight of his stare, she pushes harder, arches more deeply and sinks farther into every posture. The burn is more than that of muscles straining, though. Their next time through the sun salutation, she eyes him with a desire to do more than just correct. She wants to touch him. To feel his warmth against her palms.

He lifts up into the inverted V of downward-facing dog, and she can't resist. Breaking the unspoken rule of the yoga studio, she acknowledges a world beyond her mat, whispering, "Straighten your shoulders."

He jerks his head to the side, looking to her in surprise. "What?"

She pulls out of the pose, falls to her knees and gestures at him. "May I?"

"Sure."

Sparing the briefest glance at the front of the room, she moves to stand beside him. She places one hand on either side of his hips and pulls backward until his whole upper body becomes one long line. Even through his clothes, he's warm and solid, and she swallows hard against the feeling of his body in her hands.

"Feel the difference?"

Voice strained, he grunts out a quiet, "Yeah."

The instructor is watching them now. Lissa smiles apologetically and pulls her hands away, but the heat of him is seared into her palms.

Back on her own mat, she doesn't even try for calm. She falls into the flow of postures, but it's with a rushing, thrumming heart and with static in her ears. When the instructor cues them into downward-facing dog again, she looks over at him. His alignment is perfect, and his eyes are on hers.

She nods, then ducks her head.

The rest of the class speeds past, and before she knows it, they are moving into *shavasana*—final resting pose. Flat on her back, her mind and legs open, she closes her eyes and sinks into the floor, but the peace of meditation does not come. There is too much excitement, too much life inside her arms.

She rises when the others do, bows her head and murmurs, "Namaste." He's doing the same, only he isn't looking at her now. With heat in her cheeks, she crouches to the floor and rolls her mat. Slides it into her bag.

Beside her, there's the clearing of a throat.

She looks up to find him standing there, bare feet shoved into black, plastic sandals, his yoga mat rolled up under his arm. He's more at ease than he ever managed to be in his *asanas*. Being at ease looks good on him.

"Hey," he says, reaching up with his free hand to palm the back of his neck. "I just wanted to thank you."

She stands and slings her bag over her shoulder. "You're welcome."

"It was my first class." One corner of his mouth lifts up. "But that was probably pretty obvious."

"We all have to start somewhere."

"You could have fooled me. You looked like you were born doing that." His tone is playful, but the way his gaze rakes up and down her body feels anything but.

Flushing with heat, she demurs and waves him off. "Practice makes perfect."

"Well, you must practice a lot." He stands there, looking uncertain. Around them, the class is dispersing, and another will be starting soon. As if recognizing the imperative, he extends his hand. "I'm Kevin, by the way."

She smiles and slides her hand into his palm. "Lissa."

"Nice to meet you."

"Nice to meet you, too."

They stand there, holding hands for entirely too long, staring. Only when another instructor dons the microphone does Lissa pull away, toeing the ground, knowing she should go but lingering.

"You don't—" he starts, then smirks and shakes his head. "You probably have plans, but I'm dying for a cup of coffee. Any chance you'd like to grab one with me?"

The edges of her lips curl into a smile, her chest expanding. "Make it a tea, and you're on."

His whole face lights up—like he thought there was a chance she'd turn him down.

Ten minutes later, they meet in street clothes at the front of the gym, and together, they make their way to the corner coffee shop. He stands behind her in line and sneaks in his order after hers, places a crisp bill in the barista's hand and ignores Lissa's protests when she asks him to let her pay. "My treat," he insists.

"I don't—"

"You can buy next time."

Her jaw snaps closed, the words falling back into her lungs. It's an invitation, and with her silence, she accepts. She accepts the cup of tea, and she accepts him.

With a hand brushing lightly at the small of her back, he leads her to a table in a corner of the café. Sinking down into a chair, he's larger than life, taking up more than his fair share of space and charging the air. *Was he so* big *when she touched his hips?* As she sits, her knee hits his. She tries to pull away only to feel his palm, large and warm on her leg.

"It's okay," he tells her. And it is.

They each take a sip, and he smiles. "So you've been doing that for a long time? Yoga?"

She nods. "About five years. It started out as stress relief, but it's more than that now."

"Yeah?" He's so attentive, so focused on her.

Curling her toes, she feels the lingering heat in the muscles of her calves and thighs. "Yeah. I was always pretty flexible, but it makes me stronger. More balanced." Both in her body and her life.

"Guess I'm the opposite." Consciously or not, he flexes the muscles in his arm. "I'm strong enough, but the flexibility?" He laughs at himself.

"What do you usually do for exercise?" *How did you get so strong?*

"A lot of different things. Soccer when the weather's nice. And rock-climbing."

An athlete, indeed. "That sounds like fun."

"It is. You should come try it sometime."

Her chest gets warm at the almost-invitation. "I'd like that."

He lifts his cup to his mouth again. "It was actually one of my climber friends who suggested the yoga, as a way to limber up."

"It's good for that," she agrees.

"Would you—" He pops the knuckles on one hand, darts his eyes to the side and back to her. "You wouldn't be willing to give me some pointers some time, would you? When you helped me back there, that was really great. I was probably doing everything wrong, huh?"

She chuckles to hide the hitch in her breath and the warmth that's blooming through her chest. "Not everything." There's a moment of silence as she looks him over. "And yeah. I could do that. Sometime."

"Really?"

Smiling, she reaches out and runs a fingertip along the back of his hand. She's flexible, all right, but she's strong enough to give a clue of what she wants. "Really. That sounds...nice."

He catches her hand in his and holds it. Holds her gaze. "Yes, it does."

* * *

Before he arrives, Lissa clears the front room of her apartment, pushing the furniture aside to reveal the bare wood floor. With the lights dimmed and candles burning, soft music playing low, it looks like something out of a romance novel. Only, instead of a big, plush bed, she rolls out a thin mat. Instead of lingerie, she wears a tank top and tights.

The buzzer rings, and she pads across the room to press the button for the intercom.

"Hey. It's Kevin."

"Come on up."

Something inside of her flutters.

She opens the door to find him standing there, rolled-up mat beneath his arm, dressed much like he was the first time they met. Only a few days have passed, but the sight of his smile is a reassurance, a confirmation that everything she remembers about him is real. Tucking her hair behind her ear, she stands aside to let him in.

He doesn't walk right past her, though. He stops just at the threshold and leans in and presses his lips against her cheek. "It's good to see you again."

Her voice stutters as she answers, "You, too."

Inside, his presence is as large as it was in the café. He takes a moment to look around. Somehow, with him there, the intimacy of the room grows even warmer, the candles and the music are too much. Everything's too close.

He sets his mat down a foot away from hers and unrolls it. As he does, she lets her eyes trail over him, admiring the way his body moves. He has a loping ease to him, a self-assuredness.

"So." He sits down and slides his shoes off. "What's the plan?"

Lissa has to shake her head to clear it. For all his comfort in his skin, he's here to learn from her about a different way to move. A different way to be.

She sits beside him on her own mat. "I thought I'd just take you through my usual routine?"

"Sounds good."

"You still want me to correct you?"

His grin is winsome, even as he's admitting his lack of knowledge. "That's why I'm here, right?"

One of many. Her throat tight, her gaze cast down, she picks at the edge of her mat. "And you don't mind me...touching you?"

She glances up to find his eyes even darker than she remembered.

"Not at all." There's a flash of heat and a moment of quiet. Then gruffly he asks, "Shall we?"

She grabs the remote for the stereo and turns the volume up. It's one of her typical playlists for when she practices, the tones of it soft but energizing. For the first time, the music sounds sensual as well, the gentle rhythms of it underscored by a hint of bass. She takes a deep breath and lets it go.

"All right." After a single nod at him, she closes her eyes. "Come to a comfortable seated position."

She crosses her legs and faces forward on her mat. Echoing the tones of countless instructors and DVDs, she narrates the movements that usually bring her so much peace and calm. But nothing can slow the galloping pace of her heart. Nothing can ease the need inside her bones.

They flow through the first few poses easily. She keeps an eye on him as she goes, adding a quiet instruction here and there, verbal nudges when she doesn't trust her hands.

"Try to tuck your hip..."

They're twisted into *trikonasana*, and his alignment is entirely wrong. He shifts, but it doesn't help.

"Maybe narrow your stance?"

He brings his front leg closer in, but it's still not quite...

"Here." She rises and stands behind him. Even with a space between their bodies, she can feel his heat. He smells good, warm and clean with the faintest hint of hard-working muscles and sweat. Gingerly, she places a palm on the outside of his hip and presses slightly back. With her other hand, she cups his shoulder. Lifts.

He exhales with a grunt. "Better?"

"Much. You feel the difference?"

"Mm-hmm."

"All right. You can stand."

"Thank god." His upper half jerks upward, and he groans.

The noise vibrates through her, and she should let go. Of course she should. She doesn't. Her hand slides down his side, from his shoulder to his waist, and then, somehow, she's standing there, her front to his spine, his shirt clenched in her fist and his hip against her palm, and there's just heat. Just want. For a few beats too long, she doesn't move, and he doesn't either. "Lissa?"

"Yeah?"

"Did you want—"

It's a quirk of his speech she's coming to recognize—the beginning of a question that he swallows and then rephrases. Every time he goes to ask her for something, it starts that way. She doesn't know what he's asking of her now. And he doesn't start again. He doesn't speak.

Instead he turns around, eyes burning. She lets her hands fall away, but he catches them, holds them in his own. When he releases them, it's to ghost his fingers up the bare lengths of her arms. He curls one palm around the back of her neck and grasps her chin between his forefinger and his thumb.

"I want—"

His question this time is his lips, the gentle brush of his mouth against hers. With a quiet sound of surprise, she opens to him, melts into him. He's all hard where she is soft, and then she's falling.

In a pile of limbs, they sink to the ground, a controlled descent inside his arms. She's water beneath him as she wraps her legs around his hips and slides her hands along his chest. Just like she moved him, he moves her now, lifting one leg higher, pressing it almost to her shoulder and grinding down between them. His mouth is a rush of flesh and tongue, kissing and tasting. He slides his lips along her jaw, sucks at her neck, then nips his way up to her ear.

"This isn't what I came here for."

She pushes her hips up into his. "It's not what I asked you for."

"But I want—"

"Then do."

He proves his strength as he holds himself above her, tearing his mouth from her flesh and staring down at her. His fingertips slide along her bottom lip, probing just inside before trailing down her chest. "You're so beautiful. And the way you move... The first time I saw you, the way your back arched..."

"You were beautiful, too."

His hand cups her breast, thumb sliding in gentle strokes across the peak. "Teach me. Teach me just like you were going to."

She stares at him for a moment, summoning her courage. Reaching up, she threads her finger through his hair and pulls him down to her. Their lips meet softer this time, more gently.

He whispers into the kiss, "Teach me how to touch you."

With a surge of want, she does just that. Shows him how

she likes it when he rubs her nipple between his fingers and his thumb, how she likes his weight between her thighs. When it's too much and not enough, she rolls them over, settling them in the swatch of floor between their mats. Hovering over him, she bares herself for him, pulls her top and bra up over her head.

"Now, you."

He lifts to a half-seated position beneath her and reaches to grasp the back of the neck of his shirt. As he tugs it up, he reveals his chest to her, first the smoothly rippled flesh of his abdomen, the thin, dark trail of hair. And then there's just muscled skin, warm and gold in the flicker of the candles, and the heaving of his ribs.

She licks her lips. "Lie back for me."

Supine beneath her, he lets his hands fall to either side of his head. With a rush of power like she feels when she's deep inside her practice, she hovers over him, thighs surrounding him. She *enjoys* him.

So rarely has a lover asked her to take the lead or to teach. She takes advantage of the chance to learn.

Raking her nails lightly over the lines of his stomach and up his chest, she discovers every plane of him. He exhales hard when she lingers near the hollow of his hip, moans at a scratch against his nipple and tilts his head back as she slides her palms over his biceps and shoulders. When she lowers herself over him to capture his lips in another deep kiss, his hands move to her hips, big and warm. They dip lower, cupping her backside and palming her thighs. A thumb slips in between them, and she presses her face against his neck.

"Teach me," he insists.

"Like this."

She slips his hand into the waistband of her pants, introducing him to wet, hot flesh. He curses as she slides his fingers through her sex, and the hardness against her thigh pulses. He needs no further instruction. With his other hand cupping the back of her head, keeping her mouth flush with his, he pushes his fingers inside, swirls a thumb around her clit, and she goes molten.

Breath hot against her ear, he whispers, "I've wanted inside you from the second I saw you forward-fold."

She groans and pulls his hand from her. Rising up onto her knees, she tugs off the rest of her clothes. He takes her cue and does the same, and when she lays herself on top of him again, it's flesh to flesh, his cock hot and naked between them. Before she can spare another thought, she lifts up, lifts him up, and then she's sinking down on him.

With a muffled gasp, she feels him fill her, feels the pressure of his hands around her hips and the wetness of his lips.

"So good." He holds her flush against him. "You feel so good."

Together, they flow. Poses she's practiced a hundred times echo their names inside her skull as she moves over him, taking him into her again and again. There's the arching spine of cobra and the deep backbend of *ustrasana*.

"That's it, baby. Ride me."

Her spine releases as she curls herself back over him, arms braced against his shoulders. She rolls him until he lies on top of her, still buried deep, then bites his ear and scrapes her nails down the length of his side.

Together, they find *ananda balasana* and sphinx. He curses and grinds his pelvis hard against her. In a merging of his strength and her fluidity, he pushes her legs back as he withdraws. She feels every inch as he sinks in and in. In a few rough thrusts, he fills her, brings her close.

And then he's gone.

"Up."

He puts her on her hands and knees and grabs her hair, arching her spine to *bitilasana* before driving back home. His one hand reaches around her hip to circle her clit. The heat flows through every part of her, a gathering storm in muscles and nerves. She bites down and drops her head.

"Close," she pants.

He kisses her throat and then her ear. "Get there."

Three more hard thrusts, and she's done. Exploding from her center out, she screams his name and pulses, pleasure crushing all her senses into blackness, to nothing but the push of his body into hers.

She collapses down, slides her arms out on the wood. For brutal, blissful seconds, she gives and lets him take, until with a deep groan he throbs and stills, hips tight against her. When he finally relaxes, breathing hard, he molds his chest to her spine and kisses all along her shoulder.

He laughs and exhales hard. "You really are flexible."

"And you really are strong."

He rubs her arm and slides his hand down her torso to squeeze her hip. With a low sound, deep in his throat, he pulls away from her, rolling to lie on her mat. He curls his finger at her and grins. "Come here."

She finds a home inside the juncture of his shoulder and his collarbone, presses her lips against his throat as she snuggles into his arms.

He squeezes her tightly and kisses her brow.

"Seems like we have a lot to teach each other," he says quietly. "Yoga. Rock-climbing... Sex."

Tracing lazy shapes on his chest, she glows from the inside. "I don't know. That sounds like it might take a while."

"I'm counting on it."

* * *

She isn't very good at this, she thinks.

Reaching overhead, she makes her hand connect with a worn plastic grip and hauls herself up.

"Good, good. You're doing great." Kevin's fifteen feet below her, his voice warm and encouraging. "There's a foothold right underneath you."

She glances down to find the spot he's telling her about. Holding on for dear life, she kicks her leg out and connects with artificial rock.

He wants to take her to a real mountain soon, but for now she's fine with his climbing gym, with padded mats beneath her and a rope she can trust clipped into the harness at her hips. At least for as long as she's still learning.

In the past few weeks, they've taught each other quite a lot. His *trikonasana* is perfect now, and her climbing is starting to get better.

The sex was fantastic from the start, but they've practiced at it all the same. Diligently. And repeatedly.

"Just one more, beautiful."

The compliment makes her flush with warmth, infusing her with strength she never knew she had as she reaches for the final hold. Gripping tight, she lifts from the knees, pushes up, and with a grunt of triumph, she slaps the top bar. She breaks out into a brilliant smile and holds onto her rope as she looks down. His gaze is full of pride as he stands beneath her, anchoring the other end of the line with his weight.

"Very nice. Very nice." His wandering eyes tell her he's talking about her ass as much as he is about her climb. "You ready to come down now?"

"Yes, please."

He gives her some slack and she kicks off, rappelling down

in a slow, easy glide. Finally, her feet alight on solid ground. She unclips herself and turns and then falls into his arms.

In a low whisper at her ear, he tells her, "You look so incredibly sexy on the top of a wall."

"As sexy as you look in upward-facing dog?"

His only answer is a growl. Then his mouth meets hers in a kiss that's deep and warm.

She smiles against his lips.

Kissing is one thing both of them are good at. No instruction required.

LAST HUNDRED DAYS

Geneva King

I've got a secret. I'm fucking my husband.

Okay, I know what you're thinking: isn't that what you're supposed to do? Let me rephrase. I'm fucking my soon-to-be ex-husband.

I don't really know how it happened. Seven months ago, we were standing before the judge, citing "irreconcilable differences" and screaming at each other over who got the house, money, and condo by the beach. I don't even like that place. It's drafty and there's a family of mice living in the walls. But he loved it and anything he wanted—well, you get the point. What's that expression…it's cheaper to keep her? I was determined to show the bastard exactly how much cheaper it was going to be.

And yet, here I am fresh from the shower, dabbing perfume on my body, ears cocked for the sound of his truck in the driveway.

It's all my friend Helen's fault really. A few months ago, we were supposed to meet for dinner but then she dumped me for some twenty-two-year-old stock boy. I didn't want to sit alone all night, so I decided to take myself out to my favorite Japanese steakhouse restaurant, the kind where the chef cooks the food in front of you.

I was seated with four other people and at the last minute, a lone man joined our table. Imagine my shock when I realized it was Darren.

"Well," he said after a long moment. "Well."

Too late, I remembered how many times we'd come here over the course of our marriage. I licked my lips nervously. "I thought I got custody of all the places this side of town?"

He looked taken aback and stepped away. "I'll leave. You were here first."

I should have just nodded and let him walk away, but instead my hand patted the seat next to me. "No need. Surely we can share chicken and shrimp without legal intervention."

He eyed me warily like he didn't believe me—hell, I wasn't sure I believed me—but he sat. My mind was a mess of jumbled thoughts. I think every woman frets over running into her ex post-breakup. What you'll be wearing, who you'll be with. Who he'll be with. And if she'll be prettier than you. My fantasies involved me looking beautiful and fabulous, preferably on the arm of a new man, and him, shocked, jealous and regretful. Instead, I'm the poster child for pathetic singles, dining alone in an old sundress with a tattered book beside my plate.

If I'm allowed to brag, we did well. We didn't try to kill each other. We even smiled, albeit awkwardly. We made small talk with the other guests. The women next to Darren were a mother-daughter duo, tired after a day of moving the daughter into her first apartment. The two people across from me were newlyweds, recently returned from their honeymoon.

I half listened as the new bride chattered about their wedding cruise, but I couldn't take my eyes off her husband. The look of adoration on his face as he watched his wife talk clenched my heart.

"So what about y'all?"

The question jerked me out of my trance. "I'm sorry?"

She giggled. "I'm sorry, I know I talk too much. I asked how long you've been together."

Her husband poked her side. "Honey—"

But she continued as if he hadn't spoken. "It's just so beautiful, you know? On the cruise, there was a couple who'd been married for forty-nine years! Isn't that amazing?"

She paused to beam at us. Darren looked as bemused as I felt.

"So, how long has it been?"

The last thing I wanted to do was ruin her innocence about marriage; after all, I'd been the same once upon a time. But before I could answer, Darren spoke up.

"We got married four years ago."

Everyone smiled at us. "That's so exciting," the mom chimed in.

The newlywed lady nodded. "And you know, they say the first five years are the hardest. But if you survive that, the rest is a piece of cake." She snapped her fingers.

I felt like a fraud, but mercifully, the chef arrived and the attention shifted off us and onto the show.

The rest of the meal passed in a blur. The next thing I knew, we were crammed in the backseat of his car, fucking like we did in college. I faced him, legs splayed across his lap as I bounced up and down, his thick cock filling my cunt. I hadn't even realized how empty I'd felt until he rubbed his velvety head between my lips and thrust inside and I came harder than I had the entire last year of our marriage.

Afterward, we sat in silence, our fingers touching but not entwined, and the full force of our actions hit me. There were only a hundred days before our divorce would be finalized and his fresh come was leaking from my body.

"We probably shouldn't have done that. The judge will restart the clock on the separation."

He laughed and the vibrations sent tremors through my body. "Who's gonna tell? I'll stay quiet if you do."

"Fine by me."

He yawned loudly and stretched. "It's not like it's going to happen again."

Cocky bastard. I scooted away from him and adjusted my clothes. "Damn straight it's not."

We lasted about a week before he shattered the silence. I answered my phone to hear "What are you wearing?"

It's pitiful how quickly my panties dampened at the sound of his voice. "If I didn't know any better, I'd think you were stalking me."

"Perish the thought. Can't a man check on his wife?"

"What about his soon-to-be ex?"

"When it becomes official, I'll stop calling."

I smiled in spite of myself. "What do you want?"

"I had fun with you the other night."

My internal radar started to go off. I hadn't been married to him for so long without knowing when he was up to something. "We had sex, of course you had fun. So what?"

"Did you?"

Yes. "It was...an experience."

"An experience," he repeated. "Well...I've got this free time at lunch. I don't suppose you want a repeat...experience?"

"Wow, that's such a romantic proposal."

"Yeah, but I shouldn't waste romance on my soon-to-be ex,

right? So, how about it?"

Touché. "Not that a quickie in the backseat of your car—which could use a vacuuming by the way—isn't enticing, but you know I'm a bed and comfort kind of girl now."

He tsked into the phone and I could picture him shaking his head at me. "That's so boring. Luckily for you, I'm considerate of your needs. Do you remember the Lydia Hotel?"

Of course I remembered the Lydia. Our first year of marriage, we rented a house that had a broken...well, everything to tell the truth, but particularly a roof that leaked right over our bed. Our first anniversary we fled to the Lydia and rented a fancy suite in a hotel that we couldn't afford in the first place. I made a picnic of cold chicken and salad and then he ate me as I clutched the coarse blanket in my fists and tried not to wake the neighbors.

"Fine. But you're paying."

He sighed. "Don't I always?"

And that's how it all began, against all rational thought and orders from the judge. And all the while I told myself: *This doesn't count for anything, doesn't mean anything for either of us. Just sex, nothing more.* After all, I was about to be a single divorcee and anyone who's watched television knows the chances that I'd be getting any again in my lifetime were slim to none, so I figured I might as well enjoy it while I could.

It took about twenty-nine days for us to stop pretending that each encounter was our last. Day Forty-One, we started planning future rendezvous. Sometimes, we went to the Lydia. Once, we found a seedy pay-by-the hour hotel and pretended I was a hooker looking for a john. He fucked me as I bent over the narrow sink and tried to touch as little of the scummy surface as possible. One morning, I met him in the back of an old movie theater and sucked him off as Uma Thurman slaughtered the Crazy 88. Just as she cleared the path to O-Ren Ishii, he squirted in my mouth with an ill-disguised groan that made the other patrons look around.

Now here we are, a hundred days later and no closer to a resolution than before.

He doesn't say much when I open the door, just looks around reflectively. It suddenly hits me that it must be weird for him to be back in the house he had been unceremoniously kicked out of.

"I've made a few changes," I offer, suddenly shy.

"So I noticed."

And that's an understatement. One Saturday, I talked my friends into helping me tear down the wallpaper, and paint. And when I couldn't get his scent out of the furniture, I bought a new couch set.

"The boxes are in the living room. I put them against the wall."

"Thanks." He steps in the room and pauses. "Where's my recliner?"

I'd been trying to get rid of that that piece of crap since I first laid eyes on it. "You don't even want to know."

He sighs heavily and mutters something under his breath. "Is the toilet still running?"

"Um, yeah. I keep forgetting to call a plumber."

"Here, let me look at it."

"Thanks."

He starts fiddling with the toilet and I hop up on the counter to watch him work. He's concentrating on his task and the little muscles around his mouth tense as he frowns and I have to stop myself from running my hand over his head like I used to.

"Just like I thought, the flapper needs to be replaced. See it?"

I peer over his body. "Not really."

"Come here."

I lean over the toilet and look where he's gesturing. "That rubber thingy?"

"Yeah, the thingy," he says with a laugh. "See how it's not sitting right? That's what's causing the dripping."

"So I need to call a plumber."

"Not for this. It takes five minutes and I should have a spare here. Hold on."

When he returns, he pulls me over. "Okay, I'm going to show you how to do this. See how I take it off?"

I watch him as he talks me through his actions, his forehead wrinkling with concentration.

"There you go." He flushes the toilet and watches in satisfaction as the water stops running.

"My hero." Now I do rub his brow. "Are you hungry? I have leftovers."

"You cook now?" he blurts out, partly teasing, but mostly astonished.

"You fix things now?" I stare back at him, eyebrow raised.

"Touché, Meka." He looks at me for a long moment before following me from the bathroom. "Sure, what ya got?"

"Chicken, green beans, sweet potatoes, uh...and some cornbread."

"I don't suppose you've got any ice tea?"

I pull out the pitcher and hold it up. "Sweetened with lemon?"

"You know me too well." He takes the pitcher and kisses my temple before making a beeline for the fridge.

I'm not sure what to do while he's eating, so I sit across from him and smooth out the creases in the tablecloth.

"Why weren't we ever like this when we were married?" he asks suddenly.

That's the million-dollar question. I've been wondering the

same thing over the last few weeks. Even now, in the midst of my redecorating, he seems completely at home. And I realize that I could never have wiped him completely away because there are too many memories of him here. From the stubborn closet door that resisted his repair efforts to the curtain rod that broke after he snuck up on me in the shower. And the ghosts of our love-making that haunt me every time I curl up to sleep.

Instead of sharing these thoughts, I just shrug. "Beats me."

"I should get going." He pushes his plate away, but doesn't make any move to leave.

"Do you mind helping me with something first?" I point to the ceiling. "It's upstairs."

"Lead the way."

My heart's thumping as we go to our—my—bedroom and I show him a box on the closet shelves. "I can't get it down, it's too heavy."

He pulls out of the box and dumps it unceremoniously on the floor. "What do you need with your winter clothes?"

"I'm trying to decide what to give away. I don't wear half this stuff as it is."

"This one too?"

He's looking at the dress lying on top. It's the last anniversary present he ever gave me. It's horrid; some lurid, pink hue and the cut is all wrong for my body. We had a huge fight over that hideous thing. He couldn't understand why I never wore it and I couldn't understand how he could have known me for so long and thought that I would have been caught dead in the outfit.

He pulls it out and examines it closer. "You were right. It is horrible. It looked a lot better in the store."

"Most things do."

He chuckles. "You should try it on again."

He must be joking, and the look on my face says as much.

"Oh, come on. Maybe it looks better now."

I roll my eyes, but take it from him. "Oh fine, if it will shut you up."

The dress fits as badly as I remember, but to Darren's credit, he doesn't start laughing immediately, even though I can see it in his face.

"Nope, this is getting trashed. I can't knowingly pawn this off on some unsuspecting woman."

"Oh, wait a sec." He gets up and turns me around. "I think it just needs a little adjustment."

His fingers brush against my shoulder blades and I shiver, uncomfortably aware of how close he is. He continues fussing with the dress and every touch sends a jolt through my body.

Finally, he lets go. "Maybe it can't be saved. I see why you were mad at me." He kisses the side of my neck. "You can take it off now."

"Will you unzip me?"

He slides the zipper down to the small of my back, but his hands don't stop there. I feel him caressing my hips, his fingers sliding over the curve of my bottom—he always was an ass man. And a breast man. Actually, anything that had to do with women and sex, he was all over it.

"Meka."

For some reason, I'm infinitely more nervous than I was before. And as his mouth covers mine, it hits me. For all our illicit encounters, this is the first time that we've come together in our home.

I step out of the gown and he kicks it aside impatiently and lowers me to the bed. His mouth leaves a wet trail over my body: neck, nipples, stomach, thighs—nothing is spared as he licks and nibbles my skin.

He pushes inside of me and my cunt tingles, like she's

welcoming his cock back. I wait for the thrust, but it doesn't come. Instead, he hovers over me and strokes my cheek with his thumb.

"You're still the most beautiful woman in the world," he whispers in my ear.

And suddenly, my face is as wet as my lower half. I'm crying as we move together slowly, but it feels good. It feels right.

All too soon, my body is tensing and shuddering against his and he's collapsing on top of me, breathing heavily into the side of my neck. We lay there a while, his cock still nestled inside me, listening to the sound of the AC and the cars zooming around outside.

I don't think we should do this anymore. The thought flashes across my mind and, deep down, I know stopping now would be the right thing to do. Sooner or later, one or both of us is going to get hurt.

I open my mouth to tell him, but before I can speak, he yawns and rolls off me. "Maybe I can take a look at the closet door tomorrow morning. And see what else needs to be fixed around here."

That wasn't what I was expecting to hear. I guess I stay silent too long because he leans up and nudges my shoulder. "Meka?"

"That's fine. I'll make you pancakes."

"Sounds like a plan." He kisses my head and a mere moment later, he's snoring against my hair.

Sooner or later, we'll have to figure this mess out. But tonight, I'm sleeping with my husband.

THE PRICE OF LOVE

Kate Pearce

She felt him before she saw him, the slightest touch on the back of her bare arm, the frisson of desire that resulted as his blunt, calloused fingertip caressed her elbow. Shivers, goose bumps, *pleasure*, all in that single moment. He followed her out of the elevator into the designer level of the department store, keeping just close enough to stop any other man from approaching her, but far enough away that she had to strain to see his expression.

But he liked to keep her on edge, to make her experience him as he wished, to make her *think*. She glided over to the racks of dresses, her fingers touching and releasing fabrics, testing them, as she considered each garment, how it would look, how *he* would look at her when she paraded in front of him.

She paused at a pale-gray cocktail dress made of chiffon and silk with flowers cascading down from one shoulder to the waist. The chiffon felt fine and airy, the silk deceptively strong. He drew closer as she fingered the silk, *his* fingers now under her skirt and tracing the curve of her buttock. Deliberately, she arched her back, heard his breath catch as his palm curved around her ass. She'd worn thong panties and they were already damp.

Her nipples hardened as he traced the silk of her panties in the same careful way that she'd traced the silk of the dress.

"Would you like me to start you a fitting room?"

The sales assistant's question made her look up.

"Sure. Thanks. Let's start with this." She handed over the gray silk confection and the sales assistant walked away.

He patted her ass, stepping back as she changed direction and headed for another group of dresses, this time in vibrant reds and pinks. This time she spotted the one she liked immediately—a deep red-blue jersey with a draped skirt and a V-neck that would showcase her rather deep cleavage.

"Nice," he murmured behind her. His fingers stroked between her asscheeks, plucking at her thong, pulling it up so that it pressed against her already needy clit.

She made a little sound of pleasure as she found her size in the red dress and beckoned to the sales assistant.

"This one too, please."

"That's a great dress." The woman's gaze flicked between them. She supposed they were an unusual couple. Him in his cowboy gear, and her dressed up like a secretary, which she was sometimes, but not today. They both looked out of place in the upmarket store. "Are you attending a special event?"

"You could say that." She smiled at the sales assistant and continued shopping, her sex aching now, wanting more of his touch, knowing he wouldn't give her more than he wanted to give, that he loved to make her wait. It was a game they'd played many times, and one she never tired of.

Over to the black dresses now, shorter, sexier, tighter, but he wasn't a man who demanded that in a woman. He'd rather she chose something that made her feel good. The one she picked up looked simple on the hanger, but she knew that it would glide over her curves in a way that made him ache to touch them.

He pinched her ass, just hard enough to get her attention, to know that there would be a little red mark on her skin for him to find later to kiss better.

She took the dress over to the sales assistant.

"I think that's it for now."

"Sure, I've got you all set up in number three. It has the best mirror."

He wouldn't follow her in here. Sex in a public changing room was so tacky, so *done*, so not his style. She smiled as she took out her phone and set it to video. He'd still get to enjoy the show, though. She shimmied out of her short black skirt and blouse to reveal the opaque push-up bra she'd chosen that morning and the tiny lace thong beneath. Her nipples were already aching and she took a moment to pinch and primp them until the ache was almost unbearable. Was he hard for her now, was he staring at his phone, watching her touch herself. She imagined his mouth on her breast...

Her phone rang, startling her and she recognized his number. And then his low drawl. "Touch your clit, but don't let yourself come."

He ended the call and she returned to the video; slid one finger inside her panties and played with her clit until it throbbed, until she was wet.

With a sigh, she removed her hand and used a tissue. She couldn't afford to buy all three dresses, so she needed to be careful. The hangers rattled as she reordered the clothes and started with the gray silk dress, easing it over her head, pursing her lips so that her lipstick wouldn't stain the fabric. The silk felt cool against her skin as she zipped up the side and considered her reflection in the mirror.

Perfect.

Elegant, yet sexy, flattering and not too tight.

But what would he think?

She opened the door and walked out to the communal area where he was waiting with the other bored guys by the entrance. At her approach, he slowly got to his feet, his blue eyes taking everything in. She came to a stop and then turned around so that he got the whole picture.

"Yeah." He nodded. "I like it. Do you?"

"Yes." She smiled.

"Try the next one."

She obediently went back and tried on the red dress. He approved of that one too and the third. She suspected the little show she put on for him every time she wiggled in and out of a garment or deliberately touched herself meant far more to him than the clothes.

When she came out dressed in her own clothes he was standing at the cashier's desk chatting to the obliging sales assistant, his platinum credit card already disappearing back into his wallet.

"What did you do?" she asked, and he gave her that smile, the one that made her want to fall to the ground and kiss his feet.

He shrugged, his shoulders broad in his denim jacket, muscles straining at his blue-checked shirt with the embroidered horse's head on the pocket.

"I couldn't pick one, so I got you them all."

She felt her smile die. "That was nice of you."

She nodded at the sales assistant who was gazing adoringly at him, obviously calculating her commission and recalculating her opinion of the cowboy's wealth and status. "Can you have them delivered to Reynolds Hotel, Suite one-oh-four?"

"Of course."

That settled, there was nowhere else to go but the shoe

department to find the sharpest pair of spiked heels a woman could legally buy and use as a murder weapon. He caught up with her by the bank of elevators and wrapped his fingers around her wrist.

"Hey."

She ignored him and stepped into the elevator, but he didn't release her hand, his thumb making small circles on the soft skin of her wrist, soothing her despite her desire not to be soothed at all.

Rather than lift her gaze, she spoke to his shirt buttons. "You said it was to be my day. My choices."

"And?"

She stared even harder at the third button down. "And now you've spoiled it by buying me things, by buying *me*."

"*Buying* you?"

Without turning away, he slammed his hand on the elevator buttons, and the car stopped with a jerk. The doors opened and he maneuvered her out onto what looked like an administrative floor, which was half in shadows. She was backed up against the wall, his hands resting on her shoulders.

"Look at me."

She preferred to focus on his shirt, but something in his tone made her raise her chin and meet his blue-eyed stare.

"I'm not like him."

"Like who?"

"Your fucking ex. The guy who tried to destroy you."

"He didn't, he…" She swallowed hard. "I just wanted to have fun with you today, to play around, to remember that sex doesn't have to be furtive and negative and…"

"Destructive, yeah, I got that."

"Because that's what he'd do. Every time he couldn't come over—because his wife, or kids, or work got in the way, he'd buy me something to make it up to me." He went still but she couldn't stop the words now, the hurt, god, the *pain*... "And then I felt like I had to pay him back by giving him the best sex ever, by not complaining and just playing the part of the perfect mistress when inside me—*inside me*—I was seething and feeling like a prostitute."

He cupped her cheek and bent over until his mouth brushed hers.

"It's okay."

"No, it's not, because now I'm wondering what you want from me, what you expect, what I need to do to repay you."

"Nothing."

He kissed her again, this time delving into her mouth until his tongue tangled with hers and she kissed him back. Beside her, the elevator pinged and the wall trembled and shook as the car went back down the shaft.

His hand stole under her skirt to cup and squeeze her ass.

"You just stay right there, and do nothing." He drew her hands behind her back until her fingers were interlocked. "Don't touch me, okay?"

As his fingers slid under the damp fabric of her thong, he used his other hand to unbutton her blouse.

"Nice." He pinched her nipples one at a time and then bent his head to take them in his mouth. He wasn't gentle as he nipped and sucked and played with her. "I liked watching you touch yourself; I like touching you more myself, though."

His thumb was over her clit, circling, rubbing, making her ache and arch away from the wall. "Liked you touching this too, making yourself ready for me, right? Just me?"

"Yes," she breathed, but he shook his head.

"Don't talk. Just take what I give you."

She subsided against the wall, her fingernails digging into her flesh as he continued to play with her clit, which felt swollen and needy and...oh, god, she went up on her toes as he shoved several fingers inside her, drawing them in and out in a steady rhythm that drove her wild.

"Would he finger-fuck you like this in public?" he murmured against her mouth. "I bet he wouldn't. Too scared to get caught. Too stupid not to want every second of your time, every breath, every orgasm."

She was close to coming and moaned his name when he stopped moving his fingers. "I want all of you, all the time. Do you understand that yet?"

He went down on his knees in front of her and pushed her skirt to one side to reveal her thong underwear.

"Yeah, this, not the clothes that cover you. I don't give a fuck about those. You can return them and keep the cash, throw it back in my face, do whatever you want as long as you are happy and you need me." He slowly inhaled. "I want this wet, needy pussy. That's all I want."

She was trembling now, wanting his mouth on her so badly, but scared to speak when he'd already told her not to.

He drew the skimpy silk to one side and rubbed his mouth against her mound, his tongue flicking at her clit until her hips angled toward him and she was grinding herself against him. Fingers in her cunt, his thumb up her ass, and his tongue everywhere, bringing her to a climax that made her bite her lip to stop from screaming his name as she shuddered and shook around his skilled mouth and fingers.

When she opened her eyes and looked down, he was already waiting for her.

"I mean it," he said quietly. "I don't care about the clothes or the money. I just care about you. I'm stupid; I'm in love with you. I want to buy you stuff."

Her knees gave way and she sank down to the floor beside him. His cowboy hat lay on the ground. She didn't remember him taking it off.

"Okay."

He looked at her. "Okay, what?"

She took a deep breath and held out her hand. "We'll do the shoe department next, and if you behave yourself, I'll see if I can bribe the guy in menswear to let me into the dressing room to help you out of your clothes."

His smile was slow in coming but changed his whole face. "You're buying *me*, now?"

She leaned in and kissed him, appreciating his strength, his goodness and the taste of herself on his tongue.

"Sure, I can definitely afford a few pairs of socks."

ANOTHER CHANCE

Erobintica

"Can I start you off with some coffee?"

We've just barely taken off our coats and the waitress is right there. I can't decide if I'm annoyed or relieved. I'm nervous about seeing Tom again. We haven't seen each other in about ten years. Meeting in this little café where we'd had breakfast years before seems to lend more weight to our chance reunion than I'm comfortable with.

"I'd like a cappuccino with whipped cream and cinnamon, please." I look over at Tom.

"Just coffee, thanks." He smiles over at me. *Oh, god. Don't smile like that,* I think. He's just as handsome as ever, with his neatly trimmed beard and receding hairline. I'm one of those women that finds bare scalp attractive. Fiddling with my napkin seems like a good idea, so I slowly unfold it and place it on my lap. I lift my menu and stare blankly at it, not registering the descriptions of breakfast fare in this little old Greenwich Village café.

"You look great, Diane. It's really good to see you." Tom says this with what I can't help but think is wistfulness.

Am I imagining that? Am I just being hopeful? It's good to see him too. He hasn't changed much, except for maybe a little less hair. Still gorgeous. Still that smile. Sigh. As for me, I know I've got a lot more gray, and my middle has filled out in a way that women my age despise. I wonder what he sees in me. I decide to just accept his compliment and not argue like I might have in the past.

"Thanks," I say. "You too. I was so surprised to get your message last night and find out that you were in the city too." I had been. Very surprised. We've been friends a long time. At one point, a number of years ago, I'd wanted to be more than friends. That ended badly, with me feeling terrible. Not that it ever really started. Since then we haven't seen each other much at all. So to see him now is…well, interesting.

I'd gotten into the city in the afternoon, arriving at a friend's place with just enough time to unpack and run out for a few grocery items before it got dark. She has a cozy apartment in a converted carriage house, and she lets me stay there whenever I'm in the city. This trip, though, she's in California, and I've found it a bit lonely. When I'd read Tom's message asking if we could meet this morning, I ignored all those uh-oh feelings and replied, *I'd love to.*

"So, how did you find me?" I pretty much know, but I'm curious to hear what he'll say. The waitress comes back with our coffee and asks if we're ready to order. She leaves with a knowing smile when we ask for a couple more minutes, as if she assumes this is some lovers' rendezvous. We turn our attention to the menus for long enough to make our decisions. I'm surprised at the butterflies in my stomach. After so long, I didn't expect Tom to have this effect on me.

"Oh, I do read you know. I'd come across your name several times. A year or so ago, I liked your author page, so I could follow your progress. It made me glad to see you finally having some success. Several times I thought of writing to you, but decided not to for some reason." He pauses and stares out into space for a few seconds before continuing.

"Then I saw tonight's reading listed. I've been in the city for a week on business, probably here for another week, and at first I thought I'd just show up tonight. Surprise you. But I have a dinner meeting and with my luck I'd not get done with that in time. So, I decided to send you a message and see if you could meet this morning. Yeah, I wanted to see you."

Hearing Tom say all this makes me feel a little funny. I'd distanced myself from him after our...whatever it was, by telling myself that he really didn't care that much about me. At least not how I wanted him to care about me. I told myself all sorts of things, though I never really knew what he was actually thinking. I manage to say, "I'm glad you did," just as the waitress comes. We give her our orders and sit in awkward silence for what seems an eternity even if it's only a few seconds.

Tom breaks the silence with, "I'm sorry about Rick."

"Thanks. It is what it is. I'm managing. Throwing myself into my work and all that. I appreciate that though. You feeling bad. Well, what I mean is..." I realize I'm stammering almost, not wanting to touch the subject in this public place, yet, wanting so desperately to just throw myself into Tom's arms and ball my head off. He's the only one I told about Rick running off with his assistant right before his heart attack. Tom seemed to be the only one who might truly understand. He reaches over, grasps my hand, squeezes, and it's like I can feel his embrace in that little gesture. I look at his eyes for what seems like the first time this morning. All the stirrings I ever felt before are right back like they'd never been gone. And there's something there, in his eyes, that either I haven't seen before or did not recognize. I decide to describe the confusion I feel sitting here with him.

"Tom, you know, I've kind of avoided you during the past however many years. Not sure why. Maybe embarrassment over my foolishness and knowing how all that hurt Rick. I didn't want anyone to think *now that her husband is out of the way she can go hopping into the bed of her never-quite-lover.* And I know you didn't want to be my lover, and while you made it abundantly clear, I was so self-centered that I couldn't hear your protests."

As I'm talking, it seems that Tom keeps being about to say something, but stops himself. I realize that I'm very afraid of what he might say; that he'll agree with me; so I keep going.

"I wanted you, and when you finally broke through to me and made me understand that you did not want me, I was hurt. So hurt that I walked away from our friendship. I'm sorry. I may be making a name for myself now, but I'm still just as fucked up as ever."

I'm saved from myself by the arrival of our breakfast. Tom says, "It's okay," and we turn to small talk as we eat. We catch up on what our grown kids are doing, our work and our current homes. We've both moved a couple times since...

"Sometimes I think it would have been so much easier if we could have just had an affair. Gotten it out of our, okay, *my* system, and then gotten on with our lives. But I guess it wasn't to be. There. I said it."

I'm sitting there, somewhat dumbstruck that I actually said all that. Tom is looking at me, but not with the expression I'd expect. Though these days I have no idea what to expect from anyone. I thought I had everything figured out. No such luck. He's got this very gentle look on his face, a soft smile, and he's not squirming like he used to when I'd get all weird and emotional.

"Like I said, Diane, it's okay. I'm here because I wanted to see you again, in the here and now. Not to berate you for what happened before. You do a good enough job of that yourself."

I take in a deep breath and let it out slowly, willing myself to calm down. I'd really not expected to get this worked up. The truth of the matter is that I still want him, and that wanting makes me feel too vulnerable, too afraid I'll repeat my tired, old patterns. I want to ask him what his motives are, as if he can't just want to see me. And it annoys me that even after all this time, the sound of his voice is making me, postmenopausal me, wet. Does he know? Can he sense that my agitation is because I want to reach under the table and stroke his thigh? Why the fuck does being around him do this to me? *Control, Diane, control.*

As we finish eating, I turn the conversation to my book and the reading tonight. I'd barely begun writing when we'd had our flirtation all those years ago. Flirtation. Shit, I'd practically thrown myself at him. I'd somehow assumed he never thought of me in the intervening years, and hearing that he did, and seeing how he is with me now, makes me waver in my resolve to not get into any more messes. I assume that when we put on our coats and head out, the weather's chill will cool me, in more ways than one. I will go my way and he will go his.

"It's too bad I can't come to the reading tonight. I'd love to get a copy of your book. Signed by the author, of course!" Tom says this last bit with a smile that could melt the thickest iceberg.

"Well, if you have time, you can walk with me to where I'm staying. I have a few copies I carry with me. It's only a few blocks." I'm not so sure I like what I'm thinking just below the surface as I say this. Tom has reawakened what at times I've thought of as my monster, a needy creature that likes to be touched, that wants to be kissed, that needs to lose herself in sensation. It's been a while since she's been out of her cage.

Tom says something else that surprises me: "Any excuse to spend a little more time with you. Let's go then." He's full of surprises now.

We walk, hands in our pockets, chins tucked in scarves, past storefronts into a tree-lined neighborhood of brownstones. It feels good to be walking next to him again. It's something I've always liked. I tell him about my friend and how she lets me use her place.

"When I stay here I can pretend I live in the city. It's nice for a weekend, or even a week, though it's been a while since I spent a whole week here, come to think of it." I'm thinking of how he said he'd be here for another week, and how I don't have anywhere else I really need to be. My friend had said to stay as long as I liked. Images start playing in my head, of Tom taking me in his arms, kissing me, then...

Stop that, Diane! I tell myself that he's just being friendly like anyone would, that nothing has changed his feelings toward me, and I'm mad at myself for letting my mind wander. Silly, hopeful girl. These are my thoughts as we reach my friend's place. There's an iron gate and then a door, which opens into a roofed alleyway. We cross a small courtyard and as I put my key into the lock, I'm acutely aware of how close his body is to mine. I want to just lean back into him, but I don't.

My friend's apartment is cozy in a very contemporary way. While my abode is cluttered, full of nooks and crannies, very crazy-cat-lady, Marion's place is all clean lines and muted, earthy colors. It's hard for me to actually envision living here for any length of time, but it does make me feel sexy when I'm here.

Maybe it's all the low, horizontal surfaces. The sofa, the stairs, the bed in the loft.

"Let me get the book."

Tom stands at the entryway counter, coat still on, as I approach with a copy of my book. I'd taken my coat off and tossed it on the couch before rummaging in my book bag. I figured if I took off my coat, he would too. But it seems obvious that he's just going to get his copy and leave, rather than stay, like I'd like him to do, against my better judgment. I feel disappointed, but try not to show it. I open the book, click my pen, and smile at him as I start to inscribe it for him.

After the *Dear Tom,* I pause, unsure of what I want to say. I want to say so much. I want to tell him how I thought of him as I wrote, how I used the emotions I'd felt in relation to him—the painful as well as the joyful—to shape the story. I want to tell him that I can feel the warmth of his breath right now, and that I want him to kiss me. But I don't write that. *Thanks for being such a dear friend over the years and for being so supportive as I began my writing career. If not for you...*

I feel his hand rest lightly on the back of my waist and I become so aware of his fingertips, their heat through the cloth of my skirt, that I cannot finish my sentence. It's been so long since I felt that rush of blood, that sudden arousal, I'm not sure if I'm imagining it. Without meaning to, I whisper, "Wow," then blush.

Tom smiles and lets out a small puff of air, a not-quite-laugh, friendly and full of affection. He tilts his head and seems like he's about to say something. Instead, he leans to me and gives my lips a quick peck. We just stand there looking at each other, not saying anything. Just looking and breathing.

Humor. This calls for humor. My fallback when I'm caught unawares. Though, to be truthful, I was so very aware it's not even funny. And my thinking brain seems to have shut down.

"Mind trying that again while I'm not so distracted?" I give him my best flirty look, which I always worry makes me look foolish. But he's got such a happy grin on his face that I suddenly realize it's all right. There's none of the weirdness from before. This time our arms go around each other, and when our lips meet, we both pause, and I swear I can feel his pulse just before our lips part and a most exquisite kiss happens.

We'd kissed once, but not like this. Our tongues explore like they never did before, and this time I want to believe there is presence, intention and no fear at all. We break away, both gasping for air, and I resist the urge to start talking. Instead, I reach up and push his coat off his shoulders as I press myself against him and we kiss again. I try not to compare this kiss to my last from Rick, and luckily, time has helped fade those memories, as I've tried to live more in the here and now. But a worry creeps in. I lean back and look at him.

"Tom, this isn't just pity, is it?"

From the look on his face, I fear that not only have I hurt his feelings, but I've blown my chance of finally getting into bed with him. Just like me: never knowing when to leave well enough alone. I start to pull away, but he holds on.

"Diane, I know my behavior before hurt you. I was confused, and that confusion led me to send so many mixed messages it's not even funny. I'm sorry for that. But I'm not sorry about asking to see you today, and I'm not sorry for coming back here with you, and I'm not sorry for kissing you. I don't think it's pity that has me standing here with you in my arms. Yes, there is uncertainty; I won't deny that. But I've always wondered 'what if?' What if I was wrong to turn you down? I've not been with anyone in a long time, and part of the reason is that."

I lean my head against his chest. I'm trying to decide what to do. Part of me wants to talk this all out, but the part that knows he will be gone all too soon wants me to just shut up and go with it. I'm not sure which is angel and which is devil. Both have gotten me in so much trouble, I no longer listen to either.

"I may regret this, but could you not run off right now? Do you have the time to…" I don't finish the sentence. How can I say "…to stay here and fuck my brains out?" Because in all honesty, that's what I want. I've been alone too long and while my toys are okay, I don't want to pass this chance up.

"I would love to." Tom says this so matter-of-factly that I'm surprised. I want to ask him what happened with him in the years since our dalliance, but instead we're kissing again. His hands wander my back and I mentally follow their trails.

I've imagined this, but always in that just-sorta-kinda way that leaves room for the real thing to be better. Or at least different without disappointing. And Tom must notice the detachment that comes from my own observation of us, because he stops and asks "You there?"

"Of course. Well…" I'm trying not to break into tears. Everything we've ever said to each other is ticker-taping through my head. So much for the here and now. I feel Tom's arms come away from around me and my heart sinks. I hang my head and let the tears finally fall. Then I feel his hands on my cheeks, raising my face. He actually kisses my tears away. I'm dumbfounded. What? This is *not* the same Tom who used to tune out whenever I'd break into tears before.

His lips meet mine again, and I taste the salt. Something has broken open in me and as we kiss, I finally let go of the fear that has gripped me despite my denial of it. I had made him, in my head, something that he wasn't, and so was never really able to experience him just as he is. Now I kiss him with beginner's mind. Or what I imagine that's like. I've never been very Zen.

And yes, I can feel the pulse in his lips. I'm not crazy. I move my hands to the sides of his chest, slide them down over his ribs to the softness at his waist. I feel the smoothness of his shirt, the slight ripples of his undershirt, and then the warmth of his skin. I want to feel his bare skin.

"Let's go upstairs." I say this in a hush, as if to voice it too loudly would break some spell, and I will just have been imagining all this: this day, Tom's presence, these kisses, my renewed desire.

I take his hand and lead him to the stairs. I do this consciously, the last remnant of my questioning, knowing that if he drops his hand away, I'll know this is not the right thing. But he does not let go as we start up, turn at the landing, and climb the rest of the way to the loft bedroom. I've never brought someone up here before, and the weightiness of this decision fills me as I turn to him.

We are both awkward and tentative at this moment, as we decide where to start. There is no passionate tearing of clothes, though I long to see him naked. I reach for the top button of his shirt and begin unbuttoning with trembling fingers. He smiles, takes my hands in his, kisses them then undoes the rest of the buttons himself. In this way he lets me know that he wants this too. As he removes his shirt, I reach up and touch his chest, the few hairs peeking out at the neck of his undershirt, then kiss his breastbone. I can hear his heartbeat speed up, and I smile to myself.

He reaches for the waist of my turtleneck and pulls it up over my head. My hair flies with static, and I laugh, smoothing it down. I realize I'm not wearing the most attractive bra, since I did not anticipate undressing. But when he slips a strap off my shoulder and kisses my neck, I forget all that. I can feel the rush again, that swelling, and without thinking, I reach down and press my hand against my crotch. Yes, I am alive.

Then I turn my hand and feel for him. I'd always wanted to and never did before. Now I can feel his cock hardening into my hand and I press against his pants. He lets out an, "Ohhhh," and all my hesitation is gone. I squeeze, then reach for his belt. We help each other out of our clothes. I have some momentary shyness when he undoes the clasp of my bra and my breasts reveal their lack of youthful perkiness, but as he cups them and takes a nipple in his mouth, kissing and suckling, I find I don't care. As he savors me, I realize how much I have missed lips. And tongue. His is flicking against my hardened nipple while his lips slide back and forth over my areola, and I hold his head, kiss the crown of it with such emotion that I almost begin crying. But I don't.

Instead, I remove the last item of his clothing, sliding his boxers over the curve of his ass to release his lovely penis. I kiss the tip then run my tongue over my lips to taste the little drop they'd gathered from him. I feel another rush between my legs, and as I take him in my mouth, I reach down and slide my fingers inside myself, reveling in the moistness that I find there. I feel Tom's hands under my arms, lifting me, and we move to the bed.

We stretch out on our sides, facing, and just let our hands wander over each other's body. Again, I feel shy, but just for a moment. He caresses my curves, lingering on those places— the side of my breast, the slight bulge above my belly button, my ample ass—that I was afraid would turn him off. When he reaches between my legs and caresses my vulva, now full and wet, with the same gentle fervor, I am reassured. My hand caresses his lips, his neck, the sparse hairs on his chest, his hip, his knees, his thigh, the slight paunch of his belly and finally the slim hardness of his cock, straining toward me. Here is the proof I need of his desire.

I raise up, push him onto his back and proceed to worship

cock in a way I haven't had the opportunity to do for far too long. I am like a famished person as I use lips, tongue, hands and fingers to devour him. He tangles his fingers in my hair and I will him to pull, just hard enough. He does.

His hips are pumping up and down, and his breath is coming in gasps. I want to continue, to suck him till he spurts into my throat, but my cunt is just as hungry, and I frantically crawl till I'm poised above him. His eyes are closed, and I study his face as I slowly press down onto him. I am filled and almost overcome with emotion, so I hold still, just feeling him inside me. As I begin moving, he opens his eyes, and we smile at each other and both laugh. All this angst, and now we find we fit together so well. Joy takes over our lovemaking. It is everything and nothing like what I imagined.

We both know we won't last long, it being so long since last encounters, but we don't fight it. Tom holds on to my ass with strong hands and clasps me to him as he comes. As soon as I feel him loosen his grasp, I start sliding back and forth on him until I cry out. My orgasm comes in strong but muted waves, and I tremble with aftershocks. As we pull apart, we both lie back panting. We are not young anymore, that's for sure. I wonder if this is a beginning, or just a one-time thing. Before I can let my mind begin wandering those dark, back alleys, Tom leans over me and kisses the soft rolls of my belly.

We don't talk for some time, just cuddle and giggle. I'm not sure where the laughter is coming from, maybe from the release of pent-up years of whatever has been arcing between us. Eventually we get up and begin the separating that is necessary today. We snack on some cheese and bread. We both shower, though not together. Would that be too intimate? He has his meeting to get to and I have my reading to prepare for. We don't talk about the future.

Before he leaves, I finish signing his book, simply, with *Love, Diane* and we share just a quick kiss in the courtyard before he heads away. Wondering if I'll see him again or if I'll just head home, I go to check email and gather my wits. I change my mind a couple of times about which passage I'll read tonight. I change my outfit five times.

Later, I'm at the bookstore, talking with the owner and glancing at the larger-than-expected audience. I fiddle with my scarf, red against my gray sweater dress, a little bit of daring with the staid. I'm introduced, and as I step up to the podium, I glance out at the audience, hopeful. But he's not there. I guess his meeting did not end in time. Oh, well. I begin reading, and lose myself in the words. As I finish, I look around, and there is Tom, in the back, smiling and applauding.

After the signing and chitchat, during which he simply browsed the bookshelves, we hug, like always. I wonder if the weirdness is back, but then he asks:

"So, what are you doing tomorrow morning? And tonight?"

CUTTING OUT HEARTS

Kristina Lloyd

There's something about the butcher, and I like it. I visit on Fridays for four of his specialty sausages and during the week, if I'm feeling extra brave, I might pop in for a pie at lunchtime. Sometimes I wait outside the shop till it's busy so I can join the queue and watch him work. He has big, ruddy hands and moves with a hefty, careless grace, his striped red apron wrapped around his bulk. I stand in line, my pulse rising as my turn draws close, and all the time he's slicing ham, scooping up offal and using silver tongs to drape steaks on the scales.

"What can I get you?" he'll ask, his smile a little tired.

You can tell he likes his meat.

I want to be his meat, to be flipped this way and that, slapped on the rump, and treated with merry disregard. I do not want to be a little cake as I am for my husband.

I doubt anything would have come of it if I hadn't been invited to a screening preview at the Roxy by my friend, Ness, who's a freelance journalist for local property mags. We were having drinks and nibbles when I spotted him, glass of blood-red wine in hand, chatting to a cluster of people all smaller than him. His head was strong and smooth, shaded by close-cropped hair, and under a dark gray suit, he wore a crisp white shirt, his tie fatly knotted and colored like July skies. Odd to see him out of context. Now, without the barrier of the meat counter between us, there was nothing to leap over but the barrier of my morals and shyness.

I couldn't leap. Not me.

He caught me looking and I glanced away. Minutes later, from the corner of my eye, I saw the shape of him gliding toward us. Should I turn and smile? Would he even know who I was? No, of course not. He served hundreds of people each week. What was distinct about me?

I opted not to acknowledge him. Too embarrassing to be met with a blank expression when my heart was going thumpety-thump. I tried focusing on the conversation in front of me. He was probably going to edge past us and talk to someone far more interesting. But the size of him grew larger and, oh, holy Moses, there he was by my side, big, raw hand thrust out in greeting. I had no choice but to turn.

"Will," he said. His eyes sparkled, China blue chipped with gray.

Will I what? I thought, slipping my hand into his cool, confident grip. I feigned polite uncertainty. "Susanna Miles," I said.

"You're one of my regulars," he said. "Will. From Choice Cuts on Chessell Street."

"Oh, of course!" I replied. "I didn't recognize you. I'm so sorry." I knew I ought to introduce him to the people I was with but I hardly knew them myself, and besides I didn't want to.

"So what brings you here?" he asked.

I turned to face him more fully and told him about Ness's

job, trying not to burble as I thought of him sharpening knives in a vicious place, mists of chilled air veiling metal hooks and sheets of plastic. I didn't know if he did that kind of thing but his potential to do so made me afraid and desirous.

A young guy circling with a tray of finger-food approached us. Will passed on the offer and so did I. He wasn't the type to eat nibbles and I wasn't the type to attempt food in front of a man who made my throat tighten with nerves.

"And you?" I asked, bouncing his question back.

"We supplied the caterers at the last minute. I was given a ticket. Looking forward to the film?"

And then we were away, chatting with increasing ease, and my wedding ring was growing heavier by the second. Heavier still when conversation moved to teenage memories of sneaking into over-eighteen films and kissing in the back row. He laughed heartily at a weak anecdote I told of getting my false birth date wrong when quizzed by the cashier. I remembered Neil Wilson trying to shove his hands into my jeans as we wriggled in our velvet chairs; remembered how ashamed I'd felt to want his greedy fingers, knowing I couldn't let him because he'd boast to his friends and among them, I'd no longer be the person I wanted to be. They would laugh at my failing. I didn't mention this, of course, but the guilt and longing from two decades past animated the confused, desperate emotions the big butcher inspired.

When the speakers blared that the film would start in ten, Will said, "You free afterward?"

I had to stop myself from checking over my shoulder. *Who me? You mean you're actually interested in me?* I shook my head, blushing. I flashed my left hand. "I'm married," I said, mentally adding, *And I've just realized I haven't loved him for over three years and he and I are crawling through a desert, parched of feeling, trapped by the vastness of the time we're meant to stay together, forever and ever, till death do us part. But this, my life now, it's death, it's a living death.*

Will shrugged. "Just a drink."

I smiled. "Okay, just a drink, a quick one."

I saw next to nothing of the film. A couple fought on a stone bridge in lamp-lit darkness and he said, "I'd die for you. I will always die for you. Don't do this to me, please." Tears burned my eyes because I understood I wanted someone to destroy me, or at least destroy the woman I'd become so I could be rebuilt for life before it was too late. I remembered asking my husband, before he became my husband, "How would you feel if I was having an affair?"

He'd said, "I couldn't feel anything if I didn't know about it. Like when the tree falls in the forest and no one's there. Does it actually fall? I wouldn't know if you made sure I never found out."

I used to admire his philosophical logic, but now I think, *What a cold fish of a man I married.*

I recalled another time, years later, discussing distant friends of ours who were experimenting with an open relationship. "Do you think it'll work?" I'd asked.

"I imagine it's feasible if there's no emotional involvement, if the heart is out of the equation."

He made it sound so simple, as if you could cut out your heart, pop it under the plant pot and retrieve it when you got back home.

After the film, I said good-bye to Ness and, playing safe, met Will on a corner outside the Roxy. I didn't feel as awful about it as I should have but I guess that's the way with adultery. If it felt mainly awful, who would do it? For the most part, I was carried along by the momentum of desire, thrilled beyond all imaginings. This man likes me and I like him! And yes, as we met on the corner, it was definitely adultery, in my heart if not yet in deed.

We went to a bar we both liked but it was packed with men watching football on the big screen. "Ah, I forgot about the match," said Will. "It'll be the same everywhere. I don't live far away. And I've a good Pétrus I've been itching to open. How's that?"

How's that? Wonderful and utterly terrifying. We might end up having sex like that lonely, old tree falling in its forest. I wasn't even sure I knew how to have sex with someone other than my husband.

"I'd need to be home by midnight," I said.

"Of course," he said. "Just a drink."

Oh, the lies we tell ourselves.

His kitchen was magnificent, the sort that might feature in one of Ness's magazines: granite worktops, halogen spotlights, acres of space and a double-drainer sink. A triple row of knives and cleavers glinted on one wall, and at the room's center was a large pine table with curvy legs, its surface scored with marks. *Likes to socialize,* I thought. *Well, that's probably good.*

He selected a bottle from a wine rack, his hands gripping its neck. I hovered, not knowing what to do. When he took two glasses from an overhead cupboard, I joined him, spreading my fingers over the base of my glass as he opened the wine like a waiter, regular corkscrew and a muscular withdrawal.

The cork gave a dull pop, a starting gun for seduction.

I'm doing this, I thought as Will poured. *I'm flirting with intent. Oh, sweet whoever's up there, strike me down with a pitchfork.*

"Chin chin," he said, as we clinked glasses.

I drank, not knowing what to say. I was about to admire his

kitchen when he said, "You often look sad. You know that?"

My heart dropped. "Do I? I don't mean to."

"You mean to hide it?"

"Guess I didn't know I looked sad." I shrugged. "Maybe that's just how my face is."

He walked away to put on a CD. Sound system in the kitchen, the heart of his home. I stayed leaning by the granite counter because I hadn't been invited to sit down. When he returned, he said, "You don't look sad now."

I smiled.

"You look terrified."

I laughed. "I am."

"Of me?"

I shook my head. I felt as if a pill were stuck in my throat. I swallowed. "Of me. Of...of what I might want."

He looked at me for a long time, trying to read my face. Then he drew a deep breath and leaned at an angle, elbow on the work surface, making his body softer, his height lower than mine, unthreatening. "Have you ever been tied up?" he asked.

Hail Mary, mother of Jesus! Have I what? The room whirled, streaks of halogen whizzing past blurred granite, flying knives, swooping saucepans, and a pine table on its hind legs, dancing pirouettes among the shifting white lights. My knee bones did a runner and between my thighs, I melted like butter on a skillet.

"I..." I began.

Did I accidentally drink all his wine? Was this me? Why was I shaking?

"I...no." I pictured a joint of ham trussed up with string, its pig-pale skin bulging against the bonds. "No, no."

He smiled kindly. "I would never do anything you didn't want me to."

Never? Never forever?

I shook my head, fighting a rising panic.

Will stood, walked into the adjoining room then out through a door leading deeper into the house. Was he going to his bedroom? Was he expecting me to follow? Well, I wouldn't. I didn't think my legs would carry me anyway. Besides, wanting a wrong thing was bad enough; acting on the want could have no justification. Oh, but I thought of many excuses while Will was gone: I don't love my husband and I doubt he loves me; what he doesn't know can't hurt him, like the tree he doesn't see; how can I know if the grass is greener if I don't even try the other side?

Will returned, grinning, loops of rope in one hand, jacket off, tie loosened. "Just in case," he said, and he tossed the coils at my feet. They landed with a clatter.

He stood inches in front of me. The world froze and so did my heart. *He must do this all the time,* I thought. *An expert, and me the lamb to his slaughter.* I could see the faint prick of his nipples through his white cotton shirt. Then everything started thundering as his face moved toward mine, or perhaps mine to his. His features grew large then his lips on mine were warm, moist and mobile.

For the first few seconds, I was tense and self-conscious. My mouth wouldn't yield. I'd forgotten how to kiss. Then instinct took over and I was gone, slipping toward delirium, heat flaring in my face. I closed my eyes and behind my lids, a blue sun blazed in a pitch-black night, receding and surging. Between my thighs I grew hotter and wetter, plump tissue parting with treacherous ease. I embraced him, needing the support of his bulk and wanting his weight pressed against me. Running my hands over the slab of his back, I plucked his shirt from his waistband, my fingers seeming to move of their own accord. His body was warm and clammy, muscles shifting below thick skin as he raised his arms to thrust his fingers into my hair. Wisps of hair on his shoulder blades brushed my fingertips. He held my head still, clamped, so I couldn't escape his kiss. Not that I wanted to. His hands were good there. I fancied if he let go of me, I might dissolve into a puddle of lust.

When he pulled away, he had a new look of seriousness to him, eyes and mouth sagging, lips gleaming.

"Oh god, I shouldn't," I whispered.

Ignoring me, he dropped to his knees, hands sliding down my legs.

"I shouldn't," I said again, even quieter now.

Slowly, his broad hands rose higher, back up my legs to bunch my skirt around my hips. He kissed the skin on my thighs, making my breath flutter faster, then his mouth was on my underwear, lace shielding my pubis like an ornate gate of silk. No trespassers, please. But inside the fabric I was swollen to fatness, fluids seeping to reveal my need and welcome him in. He traced a single finger over my damp patch, making my groin pulse so insistently I thought my heart had lost its moorings and plummeted to a new place. He nudged into my briefs and I felt him, his flesh on mine, touching me where only my husband was supposed to touch. He skimmed my lips, tickling fronds of hair and when he split me open, I groaned deeply and so did he.

I couldn't remember when I'd last been so wet.

"You okay?" he asked.

I didn't answer and he didn't wait. He slid a finger along my crease, slicking milkiness back and forth while tugging down my underwear with his free hand. I stepped awkwardly out of the flimsy scraps, committed now. I heard my voice say, "No," but even I didn't believe it.

Then again, I heard, "No, oh, god, no," but it was a no of

incredulity as he penetrated me with slow, thick fingers, hooking his rough tips on my soft spot. No, it was impossible for this to feel so good. I widened my stance, elbows on the granite top, whimpering as he made magic with his fingers. He enveloped my clit with gentle, sucking lips then glided his tongue over my nerve-knotted plumpness.

My juices made a faint ticking noise as he worked me, tongue rubbing, arm pumping with escalating vigor. He didn't drive up and down but back and forth, slamming his curled fingers onto my G-spot, jerking his buried fingers toward himself almost as if he wanted to extract something from me.

I had to tell him, had to speak before I lost the capacity. "Listen, I can't...oh, god."

This was new. I felt a part of me offering itself up to him, his powerful fingers curving hard into an untouched space.

"I have to tell you..."

The world started falling away from me.

"I can't," I panted. "Please, I can't come when I'm standing up."

He moved his mouth away. "Relax," he murmured. His tongue rocked my clit then, "First time for everything."

"No," I said, and I meant it. I understood my body's ways and knew I couldn't climax when I was using my leg muscles to stay upright. "I need to sit. Or lie. Please let me. Or...oh, sweet lord."

He moved his mouth from my clit but kept pounding with his curved fingers. I leaned back heavily on my elbows, my hips sinking to meet his hard thrusts. Inside me, a spongy tenderness blossomed to quick tightness. He pumped harder, faster, making my walls grip his fingers. Then something loosened, and I was suddenly sloppy, my juices sounding crude and loud above the nice music in his nice kitchen. I wailed, unable to stop anything as a cascade of inner wetness fired a release of pleasure, the deep, diffuse reach of it melting into my thighs.

I hardly knew what had happened. I felt dizzy, close to collapse.

Will pulled away from me and looked up. His mouth was glossed with moisture. "So you're a squirter," he said. His hand glistened to the wrist and the floor was sprinkled with liquid. A splash darkened his white shirt.

I struggled to speak. Eventually, I managed a breathless, "What a horrible word."

"Beautiful to see," he said. "So horny."

It *was* a horrible word, blunt and coarse, and not at all matched to the experience it described. "I feel...that's never happened to me before," I said. "Never. I don't know what you did but—"

He smiled, obviously proud, and who could blame him?

"Did you come?" he asked.

I shook my head. "No, it was different. Not as, I dunno, not as intense as coming. Intense but not as...oh, god. Did I really do that? I think I'm embarrassed."

"I want to make you come," he whispered. He rubbed my thigh with his soaked hand. "If coming's more intense then, wow."

"Standing up," I said. "I can't come when I'm...honestly, I can't."

"Then let's make you safe," he said, and he reached for the rope.

My legs almost buckled as he stood. I'd forgotten about his rope. He laughed to see my consternation, dropped the ropes on the work surface, then pulled three foil-wrapped rubbers from his pocket. He cast them onto the rope where they shone like cheap trinkets. I winced, wishing they weren't there. You can't kid yourself you got carried away when you've put your condoms on the table.

"Come here," he said lustily. I staggered as he drew me to him with an arm around my waist. His mood changed as if what had just happened had been nothing but a polite introduction. Boisterous and carefree, he twisted me sideways, tipped me over his forearm, and pulled my skirt high to bare my buttocks. "Great ass."

He swiped a cheek with a sharp, glancing upstroke, once, twice, three times. My flesh wobbled and I squealed, shocked to breathlessness. The crack of his hand echoed in my head as he clawed his fingers into the sting, shaking me hard. "Lovely." A fourth *thwack* before he transferred his attention to my other cheek, cuffing upward to hit me at my roundest point. I was weak with hunger, ten thousand pulses galloping between my thighs.

"Now then," he said, collecting the rope. On unsteady legs, I allowed him to guide me to the big pine table, its unvarnished top as scarred as an old chopping board. He moved chairs aside and I flopped forward as directed, grateful to feel the table's solidity beneath me.

Will raised my skirt. "Legs apart." He knocked my ankles wider with his foot. "If you want me to stop at any point, say 'red.'"

Red like meat and blood and wine. Red like the color of my ass, no doubt. My face too, burning with guilty need.

Will knelt to loop rope around one ankle, fixing me to the table leg. I shivered, a flash of lucidity making me fear this could be dangerous. I hardly knew him. Supposing he turned nasty or something went wrong? What if he wouldn't release me before I turned into a pumpkin? What perverse darkness in him might emerge when I was trapped? Would he listen if I cried red?

Despite my misgivings, when he told me to raise my arms, I obeyed. He tossed the rope below the table and secured the wrist diagonally opposite my bound ankle. The rope was awkwardly long, its end flicking wildly, roughness threading through roughness as he made loops around my other wrist, working with a brisk, focused fervor. All I could do was wait, my cheek resting on the wood, arms outstretched, legs spread in display. With every touch and tug of the rope, I dropped deeper into surrender.

Will slipped two fingers inside the bond, checking it wasn't too tight, before winding the rope around the table leg. "You okay there?" he asked, voice close to my ear. I nodded, feeling soft and half drugged. "Good," he said. "My dick's so hard right now. Going to keep you tied up till I've fucked you senseless."

His words made me whimper. I jerked at my bondage, instinctively wanting the ability to protect myself. Pointless. Finally, Will ran the remaining length to my free leg, making, I imagined, an X of rope below the table to match the X of my half-exposed body. His hand on my ankle was firm as he wrapped, tested, and fastened my last limb to the fourth table leg.

He stood and I felt his appraising eyes on me. He didn't touch me although I craved his hands. The lack of contact made me an exhibit, a thing on a slab arranged and pinned for a meat trader's gaze. The forced openness at the juncture of my thighs was vulgar and shamefully hot. I felt shyer than I had when he'd crammed his fingers into my depths.

I listened to him undressing behind me. Strange that I was still largely clothed, that we hadn't disrobed and smeared skin to sticky skin; hadn't explored each other's contours, battle scars and the idiosyncratic places that make us tingle when touched. *The nape of my neck, Will. Touch me there, one day, please.*

Yet the apparent lack of intimacy in my exposure and in his distance created a deeper, more profound connection. How crazy we could both agree to act like this, virtual strangers showing aspects of ourselves others might recoil from or mock. Though I was the one strapped to a table, the vulnerability wasn't mine alone. It's easy to explore bodies, the psyche less so. We all have secrets it's safer to guard. Already I felt this man had seen a truth in me to which my husband was blind.

I sensed Will move closer. My heart and groin quickened. Inside, I was still swollen from his fingers, closed up with tenderness, thick with lust. He stroked the curve of my ass then let his sheathed, weighty cock rest in the crevice of my buttocks. I moaned as he sawed back and forth, teasing me with what I wanted but couldn't claim. I pulled at the ropes, relishing my immobility. Each loop was a cold, unyielding embrace. Being held in Will's bonds made me feel safe even though anxiety stippled my skin with goose bumps.

He jerked my hips, pulling me a few inches closer. The head of his cock nuzzled at my entrance, stout and round. He held himself, using a more deliberate approach to waggle my lips apart. He drove in with excruciating slowness, groaning long and low as he filled me with his solid girth.

"You're so tight," he breathed, and I was because of what he'd done to me earlier. My flesh clung to him and when he glided away, it felt as if my body were trying to stop him with suction. He plunged in again, pressing at my pulpy resistance, a hand on the small of my back by my rucked-up skirt. Inside me he was enormous. He thrust steadily at first then with increasing strength, making my wetness run faster.

When he dropped a hand to my clit, I was so engorged with sensitivity that my inner thighs quivered with ripples of abandonment. A shoal of tiny thrills drew denser and closer. I bleated as he rubbed and fucked, growling his own pleasures without a trace of inhibition.

"There, there," I panted, fearing he might change what he was doing.

He didn't, and moments later I was there too, poised at my peak. I coasted across heavens then tumbled into bliss, crying aloud in a voice I didn't recognize. Sensation unleashed itself, shooting pathways of ecstasy from my core to my toes.

Will withdrew from my clit and gripped both my buttocks. He thrust wild and hard, banging into my pinkness, grunts getting louder as he chased his own climax. His fingers dug into my cheeks and I thought I ought to warn him not to mark me. But I didn't want to put him off when he was close, and anyway, I hardly cared. His hands were too good. I'd find an excuse for bruises once I was back to reality.

Seconds before he came, Will grabbed my buttocks with such a forceful claw that I yelled in pain. He did it again, making me cry louder, then he was making his own noises, three distinct roars of triumph ringing in my ears like corrupted church bells. I felt him shudder as he lodged himself deep for the liberation of his white heat, hands still clutching my asscheeks.

We were still for a while, two soft, exhausted statues, then he gently withdrew.

"You okay?" he asked.

"Yes."

"Fuck," he gasped.

He set about untying me, rubbing rope marks from my limbs with each unloosening. I watched him with greedy eyes, seeing his naked body for the first time, splendid, hairy and handsome. My own clothes felt awkward and out of place, so I stripped and joined him in his freedom.

We hugged, wrapping each other tight in the glory of flesh to flesh, kissing lightly, stroking softly. When we pulled away, Will padded across the kitchen to fetch our wineglasses. I followed him, took mine then sank to sit on the cool floor, back against a cupboard door. Will did likewise.

We clinked glasses.

"Bottoms up," said Will.

I laughed. "I'll drink to that."

We stayed there for too long, talking with lazy ease, touching and smirking, smugly conspiratorial in our postcoital glow.

Then, inevitably, "Time is it?" I asked.

Will twisted round to a wall clock. "Quarter to midnight."

"I'm late," I said without moving. I sipped my wine then rested my head against the cupboard.

Will ran a hand over my raised knee. "You are," he said. "Very. We should have met years ago."

I didn't return to the butcher's for several months. I knew I'd blush as red as the meat behind the glass, as red as our word for "stop."

After weeks of deliberation, I told my husband I was leaving him. "We can't afford to separate," he'd said.

"We can't afford not to," I'd replied.

I didn't leave because I'd cheated on him. I'd cheated on him because I was leaving, although I didn't see that at the time. When the tree had fallen in the forest, I was there. I was the tree. I'd felt the break. I could hide it from my husband but not from myself.

I rented a small studio flat two miles away. When I was settled, I went to the butcher's on Friday after work, just as I used to before the fall. Will's grin was as broad as his hands.

"Two Welsh beef and red wine sausages, please," I said.

"Only two?" With his tongs, he placed two sausages on the filmy wrap on the scale.

"It's enough for one," I replied.

He plucked two more sausages from the tray, smiling to himself. "I'll join you," he said. Blue eyes twinkling, he looked at me. I smiled back, my cheeks aching with joy. Then he folded the film over the fat fingers of meat, as carefully and tenderly as if he were wrapping up my heart.

CHOCOLATE CAKE AND YOU

Victoria Blisse

Dark, delicious, tempting...all words I could use to describe chocolate cake. Three weeks into my New Year's resolution and I'm already craving my worst enemy. She's the wicked temptress who calls to me at all hours of night and day and who makes me pile on pounds just by thinking of her.

So cake, chocolate and all other things tasty and delicious are off my list of permitted foods. I'm eating vegetables and *queen-noah* or at least that is the way the health-store lady pronounces it. It looks like rice gone wrong to me and doesn't taste much better. I really, really, really want a slice of cake. A big, thick chunk of chocolate buttercream–covered goodness. But my fat ass and wobbly tummy need trimming, so I can't have it.

Not that it's any old piece of cake I'm longing for, no, it's a particular cake baked by a particular man. Ryan. The only man who's ever cooked for me, the only man who's ever really loved me just as I am, jiggly bits included. Ryan, who I dumped in a fit of idiocy just before Christmas. I saw him in our local pub the night of my work's Christmas do and he was at the bar standing next to an incredibly attractive blonde. She was tall, thin, suave and elegant. Everything I am not. She touched his arm, then he put his hand over hers. Well that was it. In my slightly tipsy going on for drunken mind that was tantamount to shagging over the nearest table so I walked over, slapped him around the face, called her a slag and stormed home.

Ryan has tried to get through to me but I've ignored all his calls and all his texts and all his everything. I've tried really hard to ignore him in my sleep, too, but he keeps cropping up with his big smile, his bright green eyes and his floppy brown hair that feels just so good between my fingers. He comes to me every night in my dreams and he's always carrying cake, *that* cake, the cake of my dreams. I wake up craving. I wake up gnawing on my pillow with frustration. My stomach rumbles and my pussy aches with need of Ryan and his sinfully delicious cake of calorific catastrophe.

And this morning when I woke, filled with hunger pains and emotional torment I looked down at my phone. On it I found a text.

Karen told me you're on a diet. I have baked a cake for you. I'll be home from six tonight please come over and have a slice. I miss you. Ryan x

Pffft. She's meant to be my best friend and here she is telling Ryan of all people about my diet. And he knows me so well, he knows what I want. Cake. I spend the rest of the day wrestling with my need. I won't go to his house. I am not going to let him tempt me. I don't give in to the doughnuts that Julie brought in for her birthday. I eat my salad at lunch and drink nothing but water all day. I type like I'm possessed, and I don't think of him and his cake. His delicious, perfect cake. I get three quarters of the way home after work then I catch a scent in the air. Warm chocolate. I can't resist anymore and in moments I find myself on his doorstep. He opens the door with a smile on his face.

"If I knew you were coming I'd have baked a cake," he sings, then with a chuckle adds, "actually I have baked for you, do you want a slice?"

"Yes, please."

He doesn't ask questions, he doesn't make excuses, doesn't make me apologize; he just takes my hand and leads me to cake.

"Fuck, this is good." I lick my lips and smile at him, "Thank you."

"You're welcome. Whatever possessed you to diet anyway? You're perfect as you are."

"Only you think so, Ryan," I sigh. My heart aches when I think of what I threw away, my dreams were not just fueled by my need for cake. I craved Ryan more than anything else.

"Laura, you've got a little buttercream…"

"Where?" I wave my hand in front of my face. He slides closer to me on the sofa and turns my face toward him with a fingertip. My skin burns where he touches me.

"Just, there," he whispers. His lips close in on mine and he's kissing me; his tongue snakes out and brushes my lips; I open my mouth and allow him entrance. I am in heaven. I can taste creamy chocolate and hard man.

"I'm sorry," I gasp when our lips part for a moment. "I'm so sorry."

"Shh," he replies, places a finger over my lips, "I believe you dripped a little bit of buttercream down here too."

"No," I mumble round his finger, "I didn't." Yes, I am that stupid.

"Oh, I must have done it then," he says, bending to the side, sliding his finger through the top of the gorgeous cake then running the chocolate gooeyness down my chest. "Silly me."

His finger trails down over my chin and into my cleavage. He smiles wickedly then kisses trails of burning lust down to my breasts.

"Chocolate and you," he says, "my favorite things."

"Yes," I reply, "I couldn't live without your cake."

He pouts so sweetly and I laugh. A real, proper laugh. I can't remember the last time I've done that.

"What? No one bakes for me like you."

"No, my love, they don't. Now let me fuck you. It is the only payment I demand for my top-class chef skills."

"Yes," I reply as he rips open my blouse buttons, "and very reasonable a payment plan it is too."

"I've always thought so," he moans. Ryan licks and nibbles my chocolate-smeared chest while he fiddles with the fastening of my bra. He's surely covering it with chocolate fingerprints, but I really don't care. I moan as the catch clicks open. He rips the lacy material from my shoulders and throws it to the side. Ryan then dips his fingers in the icing once more and slaps a blob onto each boob. He's careful to cover both nipples; he runs his fingertip around them several times exciting them to rock-hard nibs, then he ducks his head to capture one in his mouth. He sucks there for a while then swaps to the other. I'm burning with need and desire by the time he's licked me clean.

"I need more..." I groan and reach out to whip his T-shirt off and over his head "...chocolate." The buttercream is cool and deliciously greasy on my fingers. I trail them over his chest, leaving a trail of chocolate goodness that I follow with my lips and tongue. I love the contrast of cool, giving icing against his hot, hard chest. I tease his nipples then dip into his belly button as I slip off the sofa and onto the floor at his feet. I settle between his thighs. I can feel his cock straining against his jeans as my breasts jiggle at the level of his crotch.

"I still need more," I say, and I pop open the button on his jeans and gently release the zip. "I can't get enough." I pull them down his legs with his underwear and smile when his hard, eager cock comes into view.

I am glad to find there's still a lot of buttercream on the cake and pull it off with my fingers and slap it onto his dick. I smooth it all around and try to cover every straining pink inch of him. He whimpers with need when I cup my hand around him just to smooth the sweet paste evenly all over. I smile and lick the chocolate off my fingers one by one. I slowly fuck each digit in and out of my mouth and keep my gaze locked on his. I know he's thinking about my lips being fastened around his cock; I can read it all over his face. He's as desperate for me as I am for him. I still take my time, enjoying the buildup of tension and lust in the pit of my stomach and the sweet, richness of the delicious icing.

I can feel the chocolate smeared over my lips and cheeks. I know I look a mess. I don't care. All I can think about is tasting him. I drop my mouth to the tip of his erection and gently lay tight-lipped kisses all over his straining head. His whimpers grow into loud moans of frustration. I cover his cock with kisses and teasing licks. I know what he wants and I place my lips on his tip and slowly let them slip wider and wider until I envelop him and can move lower to take in more of his rod.

"Yes!" His hiss is a desperate mix of relief and need. His fingers drop to my head and he runs his fingers through my red hair. He pulls open the large clip that held them in place and as soon as the curls bounce free he captures them in his hands and pulls the curls tight. I know he loves my hair. I also know he loves the way I suck him. I smile to myself as I imagine tasting the creamy filling to this chocolate-covered delight. Another time maybe but not now; now I need to feel him inside of me. I need to make up for the weeks I've missed him. I know he agrees because he pulls my head back from his hardness with a pop.

"Fuck me, Laura," he whispers, "please, fuck me."

I nod, lick my lips and stand. I pull off my trousers and the sticky cotton knickers beneath. Ryan reclines on the sofa and runs his hand up and down his sticky cock while he waits for me. I hook my knee over him, bend and lower myself onto him. He fits me so perfectly. It's not the most comfortable fuck. One of my legs trails down onto the floor, the other is tucked up beside the back of the couch, but I don't care. I know I am where I am meant to be and Ryan is pressing a finger between my pussy folds to expose and rub at my aching clit.

"Fuck," I yell. "Fuck Ryan, I'm going to come!"

I'm always loud with Ryan. I can't hold in just how ecstatically good it feels to be joined with him. I love how he feels lodged deep inside me.

"Cover me in your cream, baby," he coos. "Come for me, Laura."

I do. I come hard, fast and wetly. He rams his cock up into me because I can do little more than shudder and shake with the intensity of my orgasm. Just as the ecstasy dips he roars and holds himself off the sofa and deeper in me as his pleasure flows through us both. When our breathing settles I push myself between him and the back of the sofa. We cling to each other tightly while we recover.

"I've missed you," he whispers between kisses.

"I've missed you, too. I'm sorry I was such an idiot."

"I'm sorry I was such an idiot, too." His voice is a gentle balm. "I should have tried harder to explain."

I shrug. "I'd not have listened; you did the best thing. You baked for me."

"The way to a sexy woman's heart is through her stomach."

He nods and rubs his sticky hand over my tummy. I giggle as it jiggles.

"Chocolate and you," I say, smiling and kissing cake crumbs from his cheek, "my favorite things."

He smiles and I finally feel sated. Fuck stupid New Year's diets. All a woman needs is a good man who bakes.

ADAGIO

Torrance Sené

Nothing turns me on more than watching Ben play the violin. There is something so wholly sensual about his performance, in the way he loses himself, drowning in the sea of his senses. His long, lithe fingers moving in quick succession, meeting the strings with the precision necessary to produce a clear, sonorous note. His intensity and passion. His wildness. Everything about him combining to pluck every single one of my strings.

So imagine my delight to hear Bach's *Concerto No. 2 in E Major* wafting through our apartment when I arrived home. Work had been positively horrid with the catering preparations for an upcoming conference still days behind schedule. My day had consisted of bickering employees, catty clients and a migraine the size of Russia. Tonight I wanted—no, I needed—nothing more than to have Ben fuck me senseless.

I dropped my purse and planner on the kitchen island and ignored the stack of mail and the flashing answering machine. It could all wait until tomorrow. Instead, I walked down the hallway to I find the door of Ben's study left slightly ajar. I perched myself against the jamb, watching the scene before me.

Sweat dampened Ben's brow, causing his wavy reddish-brown hair to curl at the edges. His eyes were closed, completely enraptured in the melody he called forth. The sleeves of his expensive pin-striped shirt were rolled up, the intensity of his playing pulling the buttons taut over his broad torso.

God, he looked amazing. And he was mine.

Concentration was splashed across his face. Every part of him focused so intently on dominating the filaments, bending them to his will; on being a channel for an ancient German master. At that moment, like every moment he spent in this rapture, I grew jealous of those strings. Envious of the way he so delicately but sternly commanded them. How he applied just the right amount of pressure, held precisely the right strand along the fingerboard, until from it he had wrenched a wailing cry. As if on cue, he brought the bow slowly across the bridge, drawing out the final melancholy note.

He opened his eyes, not at all surprised to find me there. A smile drew across his mouth as he lowered the violin from his shoulder and held it at his side. "I'm beginning to think you've developed a bit of a fetish."

I smiled back, leaving the doorjamb behind and descending farther into his sanctuary. I walked past piles of papers that needed grading, books marked with various colored Post-its, and scores of scribbled compositions—visual displays of his brilliant mind that served only to make me hotter, wetter, more frustrated—until I stood before him.

"I would call it more of a longing, a *need*."

My hand reached out, my index finger pulling back at first as if the strings were electrified. Perhaps they were, and that's what lured me to them. Perhaps Ben was channeling some mad science I could never hope to understand. My finger curved ever so slightly around the string, and plucked. A loud, deep note broke the silence; a shiver shuddered through my core. My eyelids drooped as I let the thrum wash over me.

Ben's voice came next: a lilting baritone timbre that would bring angels careening from the sky. "This longing you speak of, might I prove to be of assistance?"

I said nothing; the question was partially rhetorical anyway. I simply followed the neck of the violin, bringing my hand up past the scroll and along his arm until it rested on his expansive chest. The first two buttons of his shirt were unfastened, I noticed, revealing the perfect place for my lips. I stood on my tiptoes and brought my mouth down on his collarbone, tasting his saltiness. My hands began unbuttoning the rest of his shirt. A whisper of a sigh escaped his throat as I licked and kissed his Adam's apple.

He gave the violin over to gravity for safekeeping then, as his hands found their way to my hair, removing the clip and freeing my soft curls and releasing a waft of gardenia. He gently took a handful of hair and pulled my head backward so I faced up at him.

"Do you need to be plucked, darling?" he asked.

My knees nearly buckled as a flood of warmth spread through me.

"Yes."

His right hand unzipped the back of my black dress; the other hand was still tangled within my hair. His gray-blue eyes never left mine. "Yes, what?"

"Yes, please."

His eyes flashed with cheekiness and I shivered when his fingers trailed fire down my neck and spine. The warm flesh of his hand smoothing over my lower back, pushing me toward him. He took my mouth and I could taste the fruity trace of Merlot lingering on his breath as my tongue explored his. As my hands busied themselves with his shirt, a tiny mewl escaped my lips.

His composition had begun.

I pulled his shirt from his trousers, but his hands on mine stopped me. I swallowed hard when I saw the intense look on his face. My entire body hummed with anticipation as he knelt before me. His fingers—those long, slender digits that just moments before stirred a keening from lifeless strings—slid up my stockings, tracing the seam up the back of them and hiking up my dress until his hands rested on my ass. "I see you're wearing my favorite stockings." The corner of my mouth went up in a smirk as his hot mouth kissed the area just above my mons. His middle finger rubbed along my damp panties, tracing my slit.

I knew he could smell my arousal. How could he not when just the touch of his full lips and finger threatened to throw me over a precipice? But this was his symphony and I merely the instrument on which he composed. Far be it from me to fill in notes where he does not write them. My job consisted of singing only when he coaxed them from me.

Turning me around, he continued trailing kisses along my thighs and ass, lifting my dress farther and squeezing the soft round flesh he found there. My eyes remained closed. I was becoming lost in the moment and trying especially hard not to lose complete control and come—not before he wanted me to. Ben stood. His hands grabbed the opened sides of my zipper and pushed the sleeves down, exposing my shoulders. I found the rough touch of his stubble delicious as he nibbled along my nape. With one final shove the black fabric pooled in an inky stain around my high-heeled feet, leaving me in only black lingerie and stockings.

"Kneel on the sofa," he conducted, motioning to the couch in front of us.

The leather of the chaise lounge creaked loudly as I did what Ben directed. My mind reeled with possibilities as I propped myself up on the back of the sofa. All our past sessions flooded my thoughts. *What would it be this time? How would he make me come?* But the thing was I had absolutely no idea what he had planned. Like a true composer, when Ben set to work no group of notes were ever in the same measure twice; no *sinfonia* ever the same. This trust was how I knew I loved him, and he loved me.

I longed to look over my shoulder and at him, but I have heard said that artistry is best left to its own devices, so I kept my head straight. I saw his shadow approaching seconds before I felt his fingertips trail along the top of my thong panties.

"I've brought you a surprise," he announced.

Chills washed over me. "Have you now?"

"Do you trust me?" he asked.

"With all my heart."

I heard a faint *shoosh* in the air and then something thin and hard like wood came down across my ass. I yelped in pain, clutching the back of the sofa as the line of red-hot agony spread a mixture of pleasure and pain through my core. My scent intensified. The pain hurt like nothing I had felt before, but it was also surprisingly arousing being at his mercy. So vulnerable.

His hand smoothed over the line and made its way to my pussy. A solitary slender finger found my opening and slid in. I clenched around it.

"You liked that, didn't you?"

I shook my head yes and spread my legs farther apart,

welcoming him further. He slipped a second finger into me and curved them just right.

"Do you want another?"

"Please."

He removed his fingers and brought the thin wood across my cherry-red ass again. I cried out, and a tear of painful pleasure left my eye.

"You know it's you whom I think of when I play. Don't you?" He pushed my panties down to my knees. The air-conditioned air teasing my exposed pussy. "You, Imogen, are my muse."

I felt something cold and hard slide between my labia and back out again. "On your body alone, I could write a thousand symphonies," he continued. When I realized what he was holding, I nearly came. The violin bow. That same wooden implement with which he lures me had just left its mark upon my tender ass.

"Shall I compose upon you tonight?" he asked.

Again he slid it between my slick lips only this time he nudged my clit, and I let out another whimpering note, but this time it was sharper.

"Yes!" I cried.

He removed the bow from between my labia and pulled me back against his firm and enveloping form. His chest was slightly damp, and my nostrils filled with a heady mixture of his cologne and my spiciness. My head lay back against him as he caressed my neck with his mouth and tongue. His left hand slid into my bra and slender fingers flicked a taut peak.

He then slithered the bow back between my glistening lips and began composing his melody. He moved the bow up and down, stroking me like the bridge of his violin. Applying just the right pressure and precision along my neck and breast, coaxing delicate notes from my throat.

It was maddening. It was tormenting. It was ecstasy.

I reached back and palmed his stiff cock through his trousers. He groaned hot against my neck, and changed his rhythm from *adagio* to *allegro*. My eyes clenched shut and I was completely and utterly nowhere but in that moment. Nothing mattered but Ben, the things he could do and make me feel, and the bond of trust we shared. A crescendo of cries gracefully built within me. I could feel my climax approaching as a trickle ran down my inner thigh.

"Come for me," he whispered, before gently biting the base of my neck, calling forth a cadence to his masterpiece. And I did. My whimpers were a puling *vibrato* as wave over wave of pleasure pulsated through me. He turned my face to his and took my mouth in a deep, passionate kiss that left me dizzy and gasping for air.

"I've had your bow," I said, once I regained my breath. My hand was still palming his prick. "Now I want you."

He removed my high heels and the panties from around my knees. I perched myself on the back of the sofa, watching as he took off his belt and trousers. My pussy clenched at the mere sight of his gorgeous, weeping cock.

"You'll always have me," he said as he grabbed my thighs and held me in place, the tip of his dick barely teasing at my opening. I grabbed his face, wanting his eyes on mine as he entered me. I shuddered as his cock slid in, and I fully enveloped him.

"Always?" I whispered in question against his lips.

"Always."

NOTHING IMPORTANT HAPPENED TODAY

A. M. Hartnett

Holly had the feeling it would happen. She half hoped that the day would go by uneventfully and she could carry on with her life, la-de-da, like nothing important was going to happen that day. The other half secretly hoped she'd have her world turned upside down. That was just the way it went with John.

So when she turned the key in the lock and discovered the security system was disarmed, she took a moment on the threshold to decide whether to bring on the sugar or the spice.

She decided to go with cool. Leaving her purse hanging on the hook by the door, she shrugged out of her coat as she moved from the foyer to the living room. Sparsely decorated with contemporary pieces and boasting a panoramic view of the city, the open space that combined the living, dining, office and kitchen was as she had left it that morning, without a dirty dish or errant bit of clutter.

Everything was the same, save for the grinning devil on the sofa.

She wondered briefly if he had planned his appearance. Of course he had. John was all about appearances. Always had been. He wore a gray dress shirt with sleeves rolled to the elbows, showing off thick forearms that were draped over the edge of the sofa. His shoes were tucked under the sofa and his big feet were propped up on the black coffee table, toes wriggling inside his gray socks.

He didn't smile, not really. Instead he gave her that John Ballystone grin. One side of the mouth curved a little and the corners of his eyes crinkled. She may have even seen hellish licks of fire in each of his brown eyes.

Crossing her arms over her chest, Holly faced him and tried to reason some of her infuriation back down into her gut. She knew it wouldn't be for long, not once John opened his mouth.

"Don't you have anywhere else to go?"

"Hello to you, too, Mrs. Ballystone."

She could have screamed. Using her married title was a sure way to get under her skin. It rankled her that he used it so freely. Holly was probably the only woman married into that family who didn't consider the name an honor to be flaunted like a new diamond.

Hell, no. Being a prestigious Ballystone bride had been nothing but a pain in the ass. Of course, this had more to do with marrying the bad boy Ballystone, and not one of his timid little brothers. It would have been more practical, but with half the fun that came with being married to John.

Fun while it lasted, anyway. Now there was just aggravation.

"However," he went on as she continued to simmer, "you would never have known there was a Mrs. Ballystone given the tragic lack of conjugal visits. If I had known you'd leave me with a case of blue balls for six months I would have given you that

NOTHING IMPORTANT HAPPENED TODAY

divorce and found a new wife willing to spread her legs and give me a bit of what I was missing on the outside."

"I didn't want to interfere. If figured someone as pretty as you would find himself a nice sugar daddy in prison."

"It wasn't that kind of prison," he reminded her in a sing-song voice that ran up her spine like barbed wire and slid back down like ooze.

She turned on her heel and headed into the kitchen. She needed something stiff that would hang on until she could be rid of him. She wouldn't give him the satisfaction of belting back a shot of whiskey and giving away the true extent of her frustration. Instead, she uncorked a bottle of red wine and poured half a glass.

"So, *don't* you have anywhere else to go?" she asked, still on the fence between kicking his ass to the curb and letting this banter go on for a little while longer.

He shook his head, ruffling the dark curls around his brow. It was an improvement on the slicked-up man who had been led from his sentencing in handcuffs. He looked scrumptious, but in the same way something so sweet it would give you a migraine looked scrumptious.

"Momma won't have me unless I agree to accept Jesus, and Daddy is busy wooing wife number five. I sold the house in Miami and even if I didn't, a condition of my release was that I stay close to home for a year."

"So? Buy yourself a condo."

This time, John actually did smile. Smirked, actually, and rested his head on the back of the sofa.

"I did, and I've been letting my wife live in it for the last two years. You know, I was never one for high-rises but after enjoying this view all afternoon I have to say I can get behind this living arrangement. Fucking you with the whole city bowing down to me does sound tempting." He lifted his head and his grin widened. "Specifically, fucking you from behind in front of one of those big windows over there."

"I've done it. It's overrated."

She took a sip of her wine and enjoyed her minor victory as John's expression gave up a fraction of its smarminess.

It drove him crazy to know she'd enjoyed lovers during their separation, but at least until he'd gone to prison he'd been secure knowing that he could just show up and intimidate the hell out of any man Holly took to bed. It must have kept him up at night wondering who she was fucking while he was jerking off in his cell.

The irritation passed like a shudder, and John leaned forward and watched her drink. "Come on, Holly, we both know that if it's not me, it's hardly worth it."

"You'd think that being locked up as long as you were would have humbled you, and you'd realize that the world doesn't stop turning when you say so." She finished off her wine and rinsed her glass. "You're not staying here. I don't care if your name is on the deed. This place would be mine anyway if you gave me a divorce. Plus, I pay the bills and the maintenance fees. This condo is mine, and I'm asking you to leave."

He shook his head. "No."

"Then I'll call the police."

"The apartment belongs to me, Holly. Once that fact is established I could insist that you be removed."

She narrowed her eyes at him. He'd do it just to prove his point. Then he'd call her up and suggest they kiss and make up.

Her temper creaking up another notch, Holly strode back into the living room and stood before him with her hands on her hips.

"Maybe you're on to something, John. Maybe I ought to

move into a hotel and let you have this place. Better yet, maybe I ought to take up a good friend of mine on his offer to spend a few weeks with him."

John's brows came together. "Don't be like that."

"Maybe you were right the first time. This high-rise has no personality. Maybe a change of scenery would do me good. After all, you left me a shamed woman. My husband is a liar and a thief who went to jail for defrauding hundreds of clients of their hard-earned money. It's hard to hold my head up in public any longer."

The smile remained, but the playful light in his eyes diminished. That smile suddenly looked malicious, and under his gaze Holly felt as though she was being taken down a peg.

She was rusty when it came to dealing with John. Her claws had dulled without an opponent to spar with. John would still be at the top of his game. It was just a part of who he was.

"I'm not going anywhere," he said evenly and settled with his back against the sofa once more. "Though if you feel like you have someone better to be with, one of those talentless barnacles you manage to attract, be my guest. Take them to a hotel on my dime if you're really serious, but I'm not leaving. I've had an exhausting day, not to mention the last six months of my life spent doing laundry and mowing lawns, and I'm less in the mood for this *he said*, *she said* bullshit."

He finally tore his gaze from her, to the television behind her, and stared hard.

Holly felt wretched. It wasn't often she felt guilty about giving sass right back to her husband, but she felt the sickening feeling in the pit of her stomach now. Of course, she had worried about him while he was in prison. It was minimum security but it was still prison, still shut away from all the things and people he loved. He'd missed the Fourth of July at the Old Stone House, the Ballystone estate; missed the fireworks and fishing with his nephews and four-wheeling through the endless green forest with his father and brothers. He'd missed his mother's seventy-fifth birthday and the birth of his only sister's first baby.

And he'd missed their anniversary. Not their wedding anniversary, but the first night they met and came together like fire and gasoline. It was little more than an excuse to fuck after they'd separated, but it was theirs, and that year Holly had gone to bed alone and wondered if he realized what day it was.

Sure he was a bastard, a liar and a thief, but he was still the man she'd fallen in love with when she was sixteen and was still in love with at thirty, and she'd just thrown the worst six months of his life back in his face.

Her apology hung on the edge of her tongue, but by the time she felt ready to let it drop John lifted the remote and aimed it at the television.

In an instant the surround sound filled the room with ecstatic shrieking and heavy panting, and Holly's name on another man's lips.

She whipped around to the television she had yet to lay eyes on. Fury spiraled up and up and up as she saw herself as large as life in her own bed, coupling with a man whose name she couldn't recall in her rage.

The camera shook a little and zoomed in on her face, contorted with the onslaught of an orgasm, and panned down, past flushed breasts and erect nipples being worked by the blond man stretched out behind her, lower to where his sheathed cock pumped balls deep.

"I hope you don't mind," John said, the sound of his voice commanding her attention. He couldn't have worn a more vicious smile. "There was nothing else on television and you didn't lock the cabinet."

She made a grab for the remote. John, laughing, held it out of her reach, transferring it from one hand to the other as she clawed at him. She gave up quickly and went still, straddling his thighs.

John shrugged, pleased with himself, and worked his hips a little against her. "You could have at least sent me a copy of this while I was put away."

She hauled back and slapped him so hard that his whole body jerked and she was unseated. She leapt to her feet and took her rampage to the door.

"I don't care if your name is on the deed, I want you out." She yanked on the door handle and pulled it open wide.

Rubbing his jaw, John stared back at her, and in spite of the angry mark that was swelling up his cheek, his smile returned.

"I told you, I'm not leaving."

Holly was trapped in her own fury for a moment. She couldn't move. Her legs had gone stiff and her blood boiled in her veins. And all along John sat on the sofa like a king, restarting the home movie with triumph written all over his face.

When red flooded her vision she knew she had to move or else she'd kill him. She slammed the front door shut and headed for the stairs leading to the second floor of the studio. As she passed, the orgiastic sounds erupted once more.

"I hate your guts," she hissed at him as he passed.

John merely laughed. "By the way, Holly, who was holding the camera in this one?"

She charged out of his sight and didn't stop until she was locked in her bathroom, and then she screamed.

Locked away in the bathroom, she sat on the edge of the toilet seat and faced facts. She couldn't force John out, it was true. Not as long as he owned the apartment.

She didn't want to leave. And why should she? It was her place, she paid the bills and the mortgage no matter whose name was on the deed.

So she just sat there on the toilet lid, drumming her fingers against her thigh and grinding her teeth. Her emotions bounced back and forth between the past and present, between hating his guts for getting busted and hating his guts for crashing back into her life with his same stubborn and aggravating flair.

Spending the rest of the night in the bathroom seemed like a grim reality when the alternative was going downstairs and stabbing her husband in the eyeball.

Damn you. The truth was that she didn't hate him, but hated herself for still getting this sick feeling in her stomach at the thought of another tumult. Either she'd give in and there would be the decadence of his weight on top of her, his strength moving inside her, and when the euphoria wore off there would be bickering and fighting and it would be over again, or she'd stay closed away and miserable.

Only when the muscles in her ass started to cramp from sitting did she choose to vacate the sanctity of her bathroom and retreat to the bedroom. She locked the door, kicked off her shoes, and slipped under the covers. It didn't matter if it was still light out. She needed the darkness and the silence.

But the sounds from downstairs intruded. The minutes passed, and then the hour, and she listened to the drone of the television downstairs. Was he still watching those videos of her?

Tears stung her eyes. She wasn't ashamed. Her sex life may have begun with him but it didn't end with him; still, she didn't want him seeing her with another man—men—any more than she wanted to see him with another woman.

Frustration refused to be burned off by weeping. With a growl, she threw the covers off, leapt from the bed and pulled her robe on. She might not have been able to get rid of him, but she wouldn't suffer alone.

At the top of the stairs she was met with only the blue-white flicker of the television. Her moans in surround sound fueled her anger as she put one bare foot in front of the other and descended.

But as she stepped up behind him she saw that the video was old, at least two years, and the couple performing on screen knew one another's bodies perfectly.

They moved in sync, panting and urging, sweat-slicked skin visible in HD. The camera never moved. She remembered that day, that week in Rome, when it had only been the two of them and they had eschewed the Vatican and the Colosseum for a king-sized bed.

Holding back the breath that throbbed in her throat, Holly quietly moved to the end of the sofa and stared at her husband.

He had stripped down to his boxers. His broad chest was gloriously bare and his long legs were bent at the knee, feet planted against the floor. His cock poked through the fly of his drawers and into his hand. He thrust up a little in tune with the movement of his wrist.

Watching him jerk off never failed to do *this* to her, make the blood race faster in her veins and start that agonizing throb deep inside. His long fingers working the foreskin over his shaft, wet with precum, evoked a more sinful recollection than the moving bodies on screen—an airport hotel, his cock in her mouth, that twitch on her tongue as his orgasm reared, then his beautiful face looming over her as he flooded her mouth.

She pressed her tongue to the roof of her mouth and watched, thinking how easy it would be to carry out that scene just now, but the fantasy was quickly replaced by the need to have him filling her up. Letting out the breath she had been holding, Holly stepped in front of him and let her robe split open.

John registered no surprise. His hand slowed but did not still. He tilted his head back and regarded her, lids heavy over dark eyes. A lazy smile curved his mouth. "Hey, baby."

"John." She let the robe fall and tilted her head toward the television screen. "Did you find the others?"

"You keep them separate. I just threw in the first one I laid hands on." His gaze flickered past her for a second and his smile widened. "I like this one, though. Drunk on champagne, I think. You always turn into such a little cat when you're drunk, constantly rubbing and clinging."

She leaned down and placed her hand on his hairy forearm. "And when I'm sober?"

"You know what you want. Like now." He shook her hand off and lifted his hips. Holly carefully tugged his boxers to his ankles and straddled his thighs. "Tell me, did you miss me or is this burning off the anger?"

"A little of both," she said and arched her back as he ran his hands over her ass. "Do you really want to talk about it or do you want to fuck me?"

His grip tightened. The tip of his cock brushed between her slippery lips. He raised his brows. "Condom?"

"Never with you."

She sank down, savoring every hot inch that filled her. With her tongue pressed against her teeth, she choked on a moan until she had taken all of him, then expelled it freely as he raised her up and withdrew just far enough that the tip rubbed her G-spot.

"*Baby, more*," he said, but it wasn't the John who was fucking her now but his doppelganger on screen. Hers replied with a short outcry. Holly echoed it as he thrust deep. That perfect, hot pulsation went through her abdomen and coiled upward. She locked her fingers at the back of his neck and pushed up as he leaned forward.

Then, his mouth was licking and sucking against her throat, his large hands gripping and bruising as he tilted her back. She held on, muscles in her abs and thighs going taut as he slipped his hands to her hips to push and pull her over his dick. Together they rocked faster and faster, matching the unrelenting pace of the couple on screen.

He went forward until she was on her back against the ottoman, head hanging over the edge as he bent her legs and pushed down, both keeping her spread and using her for leverage as he pumped her harder.

The world was askew no matter which way she looked. Up, at John's creased brow and puckered lips illuminated by the glow of the television; straight ahead, at the upside-down moving picture of her other self on hands and knees, bouncing back and forth over the other John's cock.

Looking back at her husband, it appeared as though John's gaze never left her face. She was captivated. To see his expression grow more desperate, to watch the surge building as well as to feel it, hot and pulsing between her slick inner walls, took her higher with every thrust.

"*Don't stop*," the other Holly said in a breathy plea. "*More.*"

Holly reached both arms over her head and gripped the edge of the ottoman. It was an action that kept her steady, but as John pumped faster, harder, the small piece of furniture slid and rocked.

"*Don't stop fucking me, baby.*"

John grunted and released her knees. His grip joined hers over her head, covering her hands. His stance changed, feet against the floor, his weight dominating her.

"*I'm coming,*" the other John said, his voice all around her.

Above her, John groaned and pinned her. That last pass over her G-spot was the one to make the world disappear. There was only John—his damp belly pressed against hers, the flash of his teeth as he clenched them, and his cock buried deep, throbbing as he emptied into her.

She held on to him for a moment longer, just long enough to take a sharp breath before her orgasm exploded in her abdomen and rushed outward. She opened her arms to him as he sank down and clung to his sweat-slick body as his cock throbbed, every contraction sending a fresh and powerful eruption through her.

Shaking, she remained wrapped around him until one final shudder passed through him and he moved. She didn't want to let go, not of him or of the exhilaration of having him inside of her and a part of her, but a pinprick of pride loosened her limbs.

She let him go, and watched through her lashes as he toppled back onto the sofa and turned off the television.

"You never could stay mad," he said with laughter in his voice.

Holly took a moment to gauge his tone. Her natural instincts were to go on the defensive, but she was far too weighed down by euphoria to put any effort into it, and so she chuckled.

"I'm out of practice."

"I beg to differ."

She sat up and found him grinning at her. She resisted the urge to return the smile. "Don't think that just because you made me come it's going to get you off the sofa."

Still smiling, he picked up her robe and held it between two fingers. "It won't kill me, not for a couple of days."

"A couple of days?" She took the robe and wrapped it around her. "I thought it was one night."

"Maybe two. Maybe more."

She paused and stared at him. It was such a contrast to the man he presented to the world. This one, sated and smug and so fucking sexy, was all hers.

And she was glad to have him back.

She gestured to the staircase behind him. "Come on. It's the least I can do after letting you simmer in your own juices for so long."

"My, my, didn't I marry a generous woman." He followed her through the semidarkness, hands brushing her hips as she led him to their bedroom.

RENOVATE

Nina Reyes

Jane stood by the kitchen window and stared at the awakening New England landscape. Spring was still gaining a foothold in her little section of Massachusetts. It would be a while before it confidently strode on both legs. The sun dappled through the leaves of the stately elm that lived in the backyard. Nature had taken the hint; a few squirrels were playing at the foot of the tree, scurrying after one another in a blur. It was something out of a daydream.

She sighed, knowing she was incapable of appreciating a morning like this. She brought her attention back to the sputtering coffeepot, as though taking vigil at a deathbed.

The faucet was dripping. Though it was the house of her dreams, it had taken some work to get there. The kitchen was her pride and joy. Along with brand-spanking-new appliances, she had made a point of updating the counters and sink. The sink was a Kohler, a slick model that looked more like a fountain at a modern art museum. She had spent what she was quite sure constituted a small fortune on the kitchen alone.

And the fucking faucet was dripping.

Her left foot was keeping time with what was quickly becoming the bane of her existence. Jane stared at the coffee machine, as though honing some latent powers of telekinesis.

It was only seven A.M., but Jane hoped to be out of the house and on the way to the office early. This was the seventh consecutive day that she had been forced to shower and dress without the aid of caffeine. She left that task for last, grabbing her large portable coffee mug to drink in the car, despite the imminent threat that the all-too-many pot holes presented to her daily business attire. The risk was worth it. Anything to get out of the house early enough to avoid bumping into him. Life was messy enough as it is. Getting fixated on a man was one of the last things she needed. Since that Sunday out by the garage, when he was looking at her with that strange intensity and she leaned in and almost...

The black pumps were the last things that went on before leaving the house. When she tapped her bare foot, it made a light slapping sound on the tile. Walking to the newly installed French doors, she peered out to gauge how much further the landscaping had to go, now that pleasant weather was finally starting to settle back in again. Jane thought that all she needed was for the porch deck to be finished and her problems would be over. Two months' worth of renovations and she nearly had her dream home. Almost.

"God," she wondered aloud. "It looks like it could be done in a day."

Yet somehow, Garrett Shaw had told her that it would be another two weeks. That was a week and a half ago when they spoke on the phone. She had managed to avoid seeing him in the flesh for most of that time. Just a few short days, and she could go back to having easy mornings that didn't involve getting to work an hour early, braving the outside world without her caffeine shield firmly in place.

Goddamn you, Shaw.

A last sputtering hiss came from the machine before silence settled in.

"Finally." Jane said, grabbing her travel mug and putting in all of the fixings. Mug in one hand, safety lid in the other, she turned, preparing to gather her things and leave. She took a lingering look at the elm tree, which had been a big selling point for the slightly too-large house. She smiled. It was going to be a good day.

A face suddenly popped in front of the window and gave a muffled yell, "Hey!"

She screamed and took two steps back. Her arms flew up in a blocking position, her survival instincts not showing the least bit of concern in regard to the large tumbler of coffee. The shock of the hot coffee splashing across her entire upper body was enough to put a stop to her panic, leaving her gasping.

The French doors opened and Garrett rushed in. "Are you alright? Oh, my god." He took two steps toward her before the hand still holding the lid straightened in front of her, blocking his path.

"Stop!" she yelled, shutting both eyes. "Just stop!" Her exhalations were loud and her nostrils flared.

He stood there, both hands in the air in the classic surrender pose. "I'm so sorry. I didn't mean to startle you like that, really."

Jane opened her eyes and gave an exasperated sigh. Garrett was well over six feet and almost two hundred pounds of pure man. At the moment though, he looked like a repentant little boy, despite the dark five o'clock shadow that always seemed to cover his face.

"What the hell are you doing here?" she yelled.

His eyebrows rose, giving her a great view of his green eyes. "Working, of course. What do you think I'm here for?" He crossed the length of the kitchen to grab a fistful of paper towels. While Jane surveyed the damage to her suit, Garrett knelt on the floor to wipe up the mess. It didn't escape her notice that he appeared to be taking the opportunity to check out her legs. Despite the fact that the pencil skirt went to her knees, Jane felt naked. Before she could stop it, a rush of heat settled to the lower depths of her belly. The sudden sensation of moisture between her legs had nothing to do with being soaked in coffee.

She turned her back to him to put the nearly empty tumbler back on the counter. "Yes, the renovation job that I hired you for, which is taking an eternity by the way." The words even sounded bitchy to her, but she found that she couldn't care at the moment.

A loud step resounded from behind her and then: "And I told you that getting started on the project at the ass end of winter was going to slow things down, right? Not to mention the fact that you didn't care for any of the guys I tried to bring on the job."

"Yeah, well…"

He got to his feet. "Like I told you, this is a big house. A couple of—"

"Yes, yes, a single woman buying a large house for herself is lunacy, blah, blah."

"That's just my opinion and that's beside the point. All I'm saying is that this wasn't a one-man job and last I checked, I didn't have a deadline to maintain." He walked to the small trash can under the sink and stood closer to her than necessary. Even with the battered wool sweater he wore, she could make out the muscular body underneath. It was only when his eyes quickly scanned her that she came to the realization that if anyone's body was on display, it was hers.

Jane stepped back and held the soaked white blouse away from her chest. "So—so why are you here so damn early? Besides getting your kicks by scaring the shit out of innocent people."

She could see him biting the inside of his cheek to keep from laughing. She scowled.

Garrett coughed. "Just trying to keep to a tight work schedule." He couldn't keep the mirth out of his voice. "Besides, you're off to work early yourself."

"I have a big client workload."

He backed against the granite topped kitchen island and crossed both arms. "Yeah, but you've been leaving earlier and earlier lately."

Jane had picked up a paper towel and was ineffectively blotting herself with it. She stopped, slowly looking up at him. "How do you know?"

"Hey now, don't get the wrong idea. I'm not some crazy stalker or anything."

"Says the man who peers through young ladies' windows."

He pointed his index finger at her. "I was just saying hello. It sounds like you're the paranoid one around here." He stepped in front of her, far too close for comfort. "Why is that?" His hand went to an errant lock of blonde hair that had come loose from her usually tidy chignon and tucked it behind her ear.

That tiniest touch was almost too much for Jane to bear. As much as she wanted to deny it, there was nothing she wanted more than to tear Garrett's clothes off with her teeth. She wanted to see him naked, to see if a big dick went with the huge work boots that he always wore.

"Seemed like we had a pretty good rapport going on." His voice had grown quiet, more intimate than she could stand. "I meant it when I said you looked pretty that day. I hope you don't think it's just a come-on."

That's exactly what I'm worried about, she thought to herself. Speaking just above a whisper, she replied, "Is that what you're doing? Here I was thinking that you were just renovating my house."

The thought of Garrett being naked came back. She lost herself to the fantasy and nearly forgot where she was until lips touched hers. A soft exploration, a nearly virginal kiss if it wasn't for the expertise behind it. She pulled back and opened her eyes. It was the second time this morning that she had been nearly shocked out of her skin.

"Was that out of line?" he asked. "You let me know."

She was breathing hard and felt half out of her mind. The part of her brain that wanted to simply be left alone was now a lone dissenting voice in the democracy of her body. Her cunt had developed a pulse of its own. It was begging for attention, as was the rest of her. Jane was finally willing to admit that this was what she had wanted since that flirty moment between the two of them a week and a half ago. Hell, it was what she wanted since she first laid eyes on him.

Laying her hands on his chest, she balled the thick wool material in her fists and brought him closer. That was all the answer he needed. Mouths met again, but any virginal quality that had been present was now gone. Lips pressed hard enough to almost hurt, tongues sought each other. Jane put one hand on his shoulder while the other traveled along the back of his neck to his short, black hair.

With a low moan, Garrett turned them around so her back was now to the island. He placed both hands on her ass and lifted her up so she was resting on it. Hands went to her breasts, kneading them over her still soaked blouse and bra.

Jane groaned. It felt so good that all she could do was lean back on her hands and give herself to him. He brought himself forward and began to lick and nip at her neck. Jane was sure she was about to die from pleasure.

He made his way to her collarbone. "God, I've wanted this for so long."

"Really?" she asked, craning her head down to look at him. "Me, too."

Their eyes met. "Really?" he asked, a small, satisfied grin on his face.

Jane gave a small nod and smiled back. Her hands began to work on the buttons of her blouse. She wrapped her legs around his waist, kissing him all the while, stopping only long enough for him to get several layers of shirts off. By the time the blouse came off, Garrett was shirtless and every bit as delicious as she knew he would be. It was the body of a workingman. She ran her fingers over his chest and his amazing arms. Once she made it to his flat stomach and the line of hair that ran past his waistband, she knew that she couldn't stop there.

He rushed for her neck again. Jane felt him unclasp her bra in the back. His warm hands cupping her breasts felt like heaven.

She returned the favor, fumbling at his belt and pushing the buckle to the side. While undoing the button and fly, Garrett reached into his pocket to pull out his wallet. He produced a condom and looked at Jane. She nodded. She had every intention of going all the way.

The pants fell to the ground, his impressive erection straining the boxer briefs he wore. Lightly raking her nails across the front of his boxers, she leaned forward to lick and nibble his chest and neck.

Garrett moved his hands to her thighs, which were still covered by the demure work skirt. While Jane toyed with his dick, he pushed the skirt up to her ass, revealing the lacy thong beneath.

"That's some work outfit you've got there, sweetheart."

"You never know."

"No," he said. "I guess you can't." He smiled and pulled the thong down and off her legs in one smooth motion.

Jane couldn't wait anymore. She shoved his boxers down. The work boots did not lie. He was wonderfully hung and his cock was gorgeous. Long and thick-veined flesh. If it weren't for her perch on the counter, she would have immediately gotten to her knees and kissed it. She hoped that later she would get the chance to see how far she could get it down her throat.

As it was, she had to be satisfied with giving it a few assured strokes. Garrett shut his eyes tight and gave a soft grunt. Jane began jerking him in earnest, just long enough to see the pearl of precum appear at the tip, before he finally stilled her hand.

"Cheater," he said.

Jane only gave a self-satisfied smile until a hand snaked up her thigh to her naked pussy. A thumb gave a cursory stroke along the entirety of her vulva before settling on her clit. Jane's mouth opened, but no sound came out. Her hand gripped his shoulder as his thumb began to softly massage and make small circles. The other hand stroked the inside of her thigh until the fingers of that hand found her warm, wet opening.

"God, you're so wet," he groaned.

She touched her forehead to his chest. "Sorry."

He scoffed. "Don't be. I'm sure as hell not," he said, gently inserting a finger inside of her throbbing cunt. She arched forward. She needed him to fuck her that very moment. With something, anything. She could feel his finger sweeping inside of her, a delicate pressure that was quickly causing her to lose her mind.

Jane ripped the condom wrapper open with her teeth. Hands sliding down the length of him, she slipped it to the base of his cock and pulled him closer. His hand was tangled in her hair and he was kissing her as deeply as possible, still fucking her with his finger. Vaguely she realized that she was panting in a very un-ladylike manner. Another minute of this and Jane knew that she was going to come.

As though he could sense the nearness of her orgasm, he removed his hand and came forward. The head of his cock played at her entrance. Jane had run out of patience. With her hands and legs, she pulled him forward, his dick quickly easing in. Garrett gave a loud, almost painful-sounding groan. Jane's back arched and she gave a silent scream.

"Take it easy on me, baby," Garrett said through gritted teeth. His hips started working, in and out. A slow but steady rhythm built, layering on top of itself, over and over.

Jane lost herself to the sensations. Her cunt was growing hotter. It was filled to capacity with Garrett's amazing dick that was massaging and working her insides with more skill than should be legal. Somehow, with all of that fullness, her pussy grew tighter, closing in around him. She grabbed his ass and worked her hips. Even though she was practically pinned to the counter, she felt like she was the one doing the riding. It only stoked the fire of her arousal even more. Her contralto moans filled the kitchen.

"Christ," he groaned. "You're fucking wild." He leaned his upper body in, pushing Jane farther down on the counter. His shallow, sweet thrusts increased in depth and became more domineering. He pushed as far as her body would let him.

Jane wrapped an arm across his shoulders and held on. She thought that he might just fuck her right through the granite. The idea that maybe he was punishing her for making the two of them wait so long for this made her pussy clench even tighter. He was fucking her to oblivion. Nonexistence never sounded so sweet.

"You," he said, his breathing becoming ragged. "You feel so fucking good." Their bodies made wet, slapping noises. Jane was on the verge. Every bit of pleasure, every sensation and word was another drop in the bucket, a massive body of water that was held back by only the slightest surface tension. A slow wave that grew higher and higher with her body as the dam.

The force of his thrusts rocked her head back and forth. "Keep fucking me," she moaned. "Don't stop."

Garrett lifted his body off of hers to create just enough space for his hand to slide between them. His thumb returned to her clit, rubbing harder than before. Sweat beaded on his brow and chest. He worked her pussy and clit in perfect syncopation. "I want to see you come, sweetheart," he said.

The pressure on her clit and pussy combined with his voice was the perfect storm. The dam burst and the wave took over all of Jane's faculties. The clench from her pussy felt as though it went to the top of her head. She saw stars, but all she could do was scream.

Her nails found his back and dug in. His sure hip movements became an erratic, frenzied rhythm until he cried out. Face against her breasts, he yelled in time with a few hard thrusts before slowing to a stop.

Jane couldn't remember the time or the date. The year was simply an educated guess. Nearly a minute passed before her senses started back up. The feeling of the cold granite top on the back of her hand. Yellow morning light filtering into the room. It was Garrett's hot breath against her sternum that gave her the urge to open her eyes and attempt to lift her head.

"You okay?" she asked, smiling. She lightly ran her fingers

through his hair from the temple to the nape of his neck.

A loud exhale: "Uh-huh." His eyes opened and his breathing gained a measure of control. "Um, wow. That was, uh…"

"Amazing?" she offered.

He slowly nodded his head, making eye contact. "Yeah. Amazing." He rested his head back down. "One moment."

Jane could only laugh softly. As she continued running her fingers through his hair, she wondered where things were going to go from here. Things were going to be different now. She just wasn't sure exactly how.

His laugh broke her from her reverie. "I swear I'm not just falling asleep on top of you."

She smiled. "Well that's good, I suppose."

He raised his head and brown eyes met blue. She couldn't believe how incredibly handsome he was. He lifted himself off of her and then helped her up. Garrett held her for a few seconds while she found her legs again. He took the opportunity to kiss her. Jane was slightly shocked at how her heart fluttered at that simple gesture.

Pulling away, he gave her a quick look up and down. "Looks like you're going to need another shower, sweetheart."

Jane looked down. She was topless. Her skirt was still bunched at the waist and her blouse was a sad blend of white and brown with the scent of coffee still heavy in the air.

"Wouldn't have happened if some low-life hadn't scared the life out of me."

"Well," he said, lifting his pants back up. "I really wish I could pretend to be sorry about that, but I just can't." Buckling himself up, he drawled: "But you still look pretty good."

Jane had the feeling that smirk was going to be the end of her. Then she started. "Holy—Garrett, what time is it?"

He had just enough time to glance at the watch on his wrist

before grabbing both of her arms to keep her from running. "Sweetie, it's not even eight o'clock yet."

Her eyes were wide. "Are you sure?"

Garrett kissed her brow. "Yes, dear."

Even after the intense sex that had just transpired, it was the "dear" that made Jane furiously blush.

"What, you have to hit the road at eight-thirty, right? Plenty of time for a shower."

"Yeah, you're right." Jane managed to get her breath back under control. This morning was just full of excitement. "What about you? What are your plans? Do you, um...need a shower?"

"My plans?" He stuck his hands into his pockets and rocked back and forth on his heels, like a kid about to ask for a favor. "Well, I thought that you might be willing to make some room in that shower for me. You know, just so I can freshen up a bit and then get down to work. Then, uh..." He leaned in and with that quiet rumble of his asked, "Then I was hoping that maybe I could meet you back here later and, I don't know, make you dinner or something?"

She smiled. There was no helping it. "You want to cook for me?"

Garrett scoffed. "Honey, I can cook. Trust me. You won't want to let me go."

She gave a long, lingering look up and down his body before responding, "I'm sure I won't." The master bath was on the second floor, near the bedroom. She walked a few paces before turning around and adding, "Oh, and I get first dibs on the showerhead."

He followed her up the stairs.

TROUBLE IN PARADISE

Crystal Jordan

Whitney loved the way he touched her, looked at her when they were in bed. Like she was the center of his universe. He was over her, in her, but his gaze locked with hers and wouldn't let her glance away. She didn't want to. She'd never get enough of that hot, worshipful expression. It was the most amazing high, better than any drug. He'd been distant during the few days they'd been in Hawaii, but not now. This closeness and connection made her worries evaporate like so much steam.

He pressed her into the mattress, his weight forcing her thighs wider, and he sank his cock deep inside of her. The stretch made her whimper in pleasure-pain. He was thick, filling her almost too full, but she wanted more. Running her hands down the flexing muscles of his back, she dug her nails into his ass to urge him on.

"Hurry, Drew," she whispered. Yes, she wanted him hard and fast and so deep she couldn't tell where he ended and she began. Maybe then she could pretend this trip to paradise was as perfect as she'd hoped it would be. She squeezed her eyes shut and stuffed the thought away into the darkest corner of her soul.

The sharp nip of his teeth on her shoulder made her jolt, and her gaze flew to his. The corners of his eyes crinkled. "I think I lost you there for a moment. Am I boring you?"

Rotating his hips, he ground down on her clitoris, making her pussy flood with juices, and she sobbed on a breath. Her legs cinched around his waist, and she moved with him. His thrusts picked up speed and force, and sensations swamped her. The hair on his chest rasped her nipples every time he penetrated her; sweat made their bodies slide together. The bed creaked beneath them, and the sound of their panting breath and low moans created a carnal symphony in the hotel room. She could feel orgasm building, tightening her inner muscles until she was close to breaking. Each time he pressed his dick into her pussy it pushed her toward that inevitable end.

He grasped her knee, pulling her leg higher so he could fuck her harder. She cried out, arching into him as she shattered into a million pieces. Her sex contracted around his cock, milking the length of him as climax dragged her under. "Drew!"

"Whitney." He breathed the word like a prayer, burying his face in the crook of her neck. He sank deep inside of her, his big body locking tight as he jetted come into her pussy.

She shivered as the air-conditioning kicked on, and held him closer. It took long minutes for her heart rate and breathing to return to normal. She sighed, contentment drowning out the worry, for now. Trailing her fingers over the sweat-dampened skin of his shoulders, she tried to hold on to the moment. "This is perfect."

"Yeah...perfect," he repeated, but there was an odd inflection to his voice. He kissed her throat and lifted away from her.

Rolling to his side, he left her staring at the wall of his back.

The gesture gutted her. Pain twisted like a knife in her heart. When had Drew *ever* turned away from her after sex? Maybe it shouldn't bother her, but it did. She set a hand on his arm, and the muscles twitched as if he wanted to avoid her touch. Moisture burned the backs of her eyes, but she blinked the tears away.

"Drew, are you sure everything's all right?" She was starting to feel like a broken record, she'd asked the question so many times since they'd arrived in Honolulu. Knots formed in her belly, confusion and hurt warring for dominance within her. They'd both been so excited to come here, to get away for a whole week together. She had no idea what had changed, and his keeping things from her and refusing to talk just didn't happen. Not once in the four years they'd been together. It wasn't like him, and it scared her. She didn't even know how to react. Should she push harder? Back off and let him sort out whatever was wrong on his own?

He sighed, the sound impatient. "I'm fine, honey. How many times do I have to say it?"

Swallowing the sharp retort that hovered on the tip of her tongue, she clamped her mouth shut. It wouldn't help. She'd tried arguing, cajoling and reasoning the last few days, but he wasn't budging. Things were not *fine*, no matter what he said. The tension and uncertainty built within her until she wanted to scream. She couldn't stay here, looking at his back and wondering if this sudden distance between them was going to become permanent. God, what a nightmare. She jerked upright in bed, scooted over to the side so she could stand and found her legs were so shaky they didn't want to hold her. She gritted her teeth, locked her knees and forced herself to keep going. To where, she wasn't sure, but she couldn't be in this room right now.

Rummaging through her open suitcase, she found her fingers

tangling in the strings of her bikini top. She picked it up and tied it on, found the bottom and slid that on too. Good enough.

She heard Drew stir on the sheets. "Where are you going?"

"Swimming."

He made an incredulous noise. "It's dark outside."

"They have a pool that's open until ten. I won't be long." Just long enough to clear her head and get a grip on her emotions. She turned for the door and walked out.

But she didn't go to one of the many pools at the Hilton Hawaiian Village. There were people there and she didn't want to deal with them. Instead, she walked toward the rolling crash of ocean waves until she stood on the beach. For once, it was deserted. She could hear the sound of music and people coming from the hotel restaurants, but the noise faded the closer she got to the surf. She went to very edge of the waterline, passing a few torches that made firelight dance across the sand. She sat just beyond the reach of the waves and let the warm breeze and darkness envelop her.

What was going on? That was the question she couldn't answer and that Drew was evading. Things had been *good* between them for four years. They'd had their ups and downs, but they'd both been willing to work out any problems. They'd never avoided an issue before. So why was he avoiding one now? Was the problem so big they couldn't overcome it this time? The very idea sent dread spiraling through her. She pulled her legs to her chest, wrapped her arms around them and pressed her forehead on the bony plateau of her knees. It wasn't just the fear of losing him that squeezed tight around her heart, but also…anger. It simmered in her blood, made her want to lash out. How could he have let something come between them without telling her what was wrong?

Some tiny part of her had thought—hoped—that Drew might

actually ask her to marry him on this trip. A laugh escaped her, and it tripped over a sob. Wow, had she been wrong. She loved him so much, had since their first date, if she was baldly honest. The feeling had only grown stronger with time. She didn't want to lose that. A week ago, the possibility wouldn't even have crossed her mind. But, now? Now, she didn't know anything.

"Hey."

She jolted at the sound of his voice behind her, twisting around to look up at him. "What are you doing here?"

"I could ask you the same thing. This isn't the pool." His footsteps crunched in the sand, and then he lowered himself down to sit beside her. Close, but not close enough to touch. He didn't look at her, didn't speak for a long moment, just stared out over the water.

He cleared his throat. "I'm not fine."

The words were quiet, but she heard them. Relief and terror ricocheted through her. She was finally going to get her answers, but after days of buildup, she wasn't sure she could handle how badly the truth might hurt. She shut her eyes tight for a moment, bracing herself for what might be a killing blow. "I know."

Picking up a handful of sand, he let it slip through his fingers. "I don't even know how to say what I need to say."

"Is there someone else?" There. Her worst fear, out in the open. The one problem there was absolutely no fixing. The deal-breaker. God help her, she didn't think she could live with that. It would destroy something deep inside of her if this man she trusted with her life, her very soul, had cheated on her.

"*No!*" His voice sharpened with shock. "Jesus Christ, do you really think I could do that to you? To *us?*"

She huffed out a laugh to cover the moisture that glutted her eyes. "I don't know what to think. I just know you're keeping things from me, lying to me about everything being all right."

A wayward tear streaked down her cheek, cooled by the ocean breeze. "I wish we'd never come here. I thought you were going to—" She cut herself off, brushing the tear away. "It doesn't matter what I thought. Hawaii was a mistake, clearly."

"No, it wasn't." The backs of his knuckles stroked down the side of her arm, the first time he'd initiated any kind of contact since they'd arrived. Goose bumps raised on her skin, a small spark of heat flashing through her. She'd have to be dead not to react to this man, which she used to think was a good thing. At the moment, she wasn't so sure.

"It really was." She shook her head. "I want to go home."

His clothing rustled as he resettled on the sand, his shoulder brushing hers. He wasn't wearing a shirt, just swim trunks, so even that small brush of his skin against hers made her shiver in awareness. She heard something creak, and then he set something down between them. Squinting in the dark, it took her a moment to make out what it was, and then moonlight made it sparkle. An open ring box. With a gorgeous diamond ring in it.

She stared at it blankly for a long moment. "I don't understand."

"You said, 'I thought you were going to' and then you stopped. Propose. You thought I was going to propose." He caught her hand, squeezing her limp fingers. "Right?"

Emotions cinched her chest, so many of them churning inside of her that she couldn't even sort them all out. This was crazy. Utterly insane. "And that's why you've been acting like you can't stand me? Because you want to marry me?"

He flinched, but didn't deny it. "No. That's not why."

"Then, *why?*" Snatching her fingers away from him, she hugged her arms around her torso. "Why would you do that to me? Do you know how scared I've been, how worried? I've been going out of my mind trying to figure out what happened, and you wouldn't talk to me, and kept acting like I was insane for asking what was wrong." She clamped a hand over her mouth, willing the tears not to fall.

He scooped her into his lap, easily overpowering any escape attempts. Resting his chin on the top of her head, he held her close. It felt good to be in his arms, and she hated that. She wanted to curl into his comforting, familiar warmth, and at the same time she wanted to shove him away. He stroked his fingers through her hair. "I'm sorry, Whitney. I've been an ass. There's no excuse good enough for my behavior."

"Just tell me why." There had to be a reason. The man she loved wouldn't act like this without a reason. And it had better be a damn good one.

"The day before we left, I picked the ring up from the jeweler's on my lunch break. I had the whole thing planned out. Dinner at the Royal Hawaiian on our last night here, a table overlooking the ocean, and I was going to ask you. I thought it'd be something you'd really love."

It would have been. She laid her head on his chest and wished it had turned out the way he'd described. Too late now, but it would have been...perfect.

He sighed. "So I was at my desk, I'd just made the dinner reservations, and I took a last look at the ring to make sure it was exactly the way I ordered it. I was nervous as hell, trying to think about how I'd ask—down on one knee or maybe that wouldn't work in the restaurant, stuff like that. Mostly, I was hoping I didn't fuck it up and say it wrong. I *wanted* to get this right for you—I wanted it to be something you'd remember and tell our grandkids about." Self-derision underscored his tone, as if he knew that he'd already blown his shot at getting it right. "Then Jim walked into my office."

"Ah." She wasn't sure how that fit into anything, so she asked the same thing she asked any time he brought up Jim. "How's his wife?"

The man had worked with Drew for years, and Whitney had made small talk with his wife at all the holiday parties and the annual retreats where significant others were invited.

Drew snorted. "Divorcing him, that's how she is. She hooked up with their mailman and moved out."

"Ouch."

"Yeah." He squeezed her tight, compressing her ribs. "So, I sit there with the ring in my hand while Jim starts sobbing about his wife leaving him. He tells me I shouldn't get married, that things were perfect for them before they got married. All I'd be doing was screwing up a good thing, because look at what happened to him. In five years, you'd be fucking around with the mailman too, and I'd be alone and miserable."

Holy shit. He'd been walking around thinking this for *days*? She wanted to soothe him and smack some sense into him at the same time. "Drew, if I were so unhappy in our relationship that I wanted to go elsewhere, you would know. I'm not exactly subtle when I think we need to talk about something. I tell you. I ask when I suspect something is wrong. If we were in trouble and I was leaving, it wouldn't be some big shock to you. I would *never*—"

"I know." He kissed her forehead. "I *know* it's insane, I really do. You're not his wife, and I'm not him."

She blew out a breath, trying to look beyond her emotions and see his side. "But he got to you because you were already nervous and he gave you a big reason to doubt."

"That sums it up nicely, yeah." He traced the lines of her bikini ties, and a frisson of awareness ran through her. "So I've been trying to figure out what to do the last couple of days.

Should I go through with proposing, or call it off and pretend I'd never considered it? Because the last thing I want is for you to walk away. That's what sent me into such a tailspin. The idea that marriage might do something to mess up this amazing thing we have. That *anything* might mess it up scared the piss out of me. I never want to lose you, Whitney."

"I never intended to go anywhere. Marriage proposal or not. I was hoping you would ask, but if you didn't…" She shrugged, tried for a wobbly smile. "I was just excited to get a week in Hawaii with you. It was supposed to be a dream vacation."

"Yeah, and I killed that for you. I'm so fucking sorry, honey." He brushed a kiss over her temple, her earlobe, her jaw. Then he sighed and dropped his forehead against hers. "Watching you walk out after sex was a pretty clarifying moment for me."

The pain in his voice made her wince. "I freaked out. You turned your back on me and wouldn't tell me what was wr—"

His arms tightened around her, cutting her off. His tone was harsh with self-disgust when he spoke. "It was a wake-up call I needed—one that I deserved. I've been doing a damn good job of pushing you away, which makes no sense when all I want is for you to stay." He snorted. "I've been a complete idiot, and I'm sorry."

The disquiet that had hounded her finally released its grip, and she drew the first easy breath in days. She slid her arms around his waist but leaned back to meet his gaze. It was as clear and open as she was used to, no more shadows, no more secrets. "You explained why, which is what I needed."

A muscle ticked in his jaw, and he shook his head. "It's still no excuse. I should never have let Jim shake me. And I hurt you in the process."

"Well, while you're busy beating yourself up, I'll forgive you." She grinned up at him. As long as she knew they were all right, that was all she really cared about. It was enough. They'd figure the rest of it out later.

He bracketed her chin with his hand, forcing her to meet his serious gaze. "I love you, Whitney. And I do want to get married. I want that commitment with you—kids, grandkids, everything." His smile was lopsided. "I understand if you need to think about it first, since I haven't really given you any good reasons to say yes lately, but I know what I want, and you should know that. I'm all in. Forever."

Tears backed up in her eyes, and her lips trembled. This was exactly the kind of thing she'd hoped he would say when they came here, and it felt just as amazing as she'd imagined. It had been a little rocky getting to this moment, but it was pretty damn wonderful. "Me, too. To all of that. I'm in. I want the kids, the ring, and everything else. Just promise you'll never scare me like this again. We have to *talk* to each other if there's an issue."

"I promise. I've never done this before, and I don't plan to make a habit of it. I'm sorry I scared you." He pressed a small kiss to her lips, and she leaned into him to deepen the contact. Groaning, he feasted on her mouth as if he were a starving man. He thrust his tongue between her lips, and heat spiraled within her. She curled her arms around his neck, reveling in the press of his bare flesh against hers. Their bathing suits didn't cover much, and she took advantage of that, rubbing her torso against his. Her nipples tightened in her bikini top, the friction stimulating them into hard points. She welcomed the reaction, the chemistry between them, glad they'd overcome the crisis and could get back on level footing again. Maybe even take the big step forward she'd been hoping for. Apparently, he'd been hoping for the same. She smiled against his lips as euphoria hit her. Everything was going to be all right. They were in love and wanted to marry each other. She couldn't ask for more.

He broke the kiss to come up for air. "So, was that a yes?"

"Hmm?" She traced his lower lip with her tongue.

"You said you're in." He pushed his hand into her hair, tugging her head back so she'd look at him. Hope and uncertainty shone in his gaze. "Does that mean...you'll marry me? Even though I screwed up the proposal and I've been a jerk since we got here?"

"Yes." A smile quirked the corners of her mouth. "Because even though you messed up, you came to me and apologized and promised not to do it again. We all make mistakes, but it's what we do about them that makes a difference. You acknowledged it and did what you could to fix it. That's all I need." She cupped a hand over his jaw, and he leaned into her palm. "In the end, you've had four years of awesome and a handful of days of butt-head. Your track record wins out."

He chuckled and turned his head to kiss the base of her thumb. She grinned at him, feeling contentment wrap around her soul, soothing the hurt. "I love you and I want to be with you. So, yes. I'll marry you."

"I love you so damn much." He kissed her, hard and fast, and then pulled back. Bending to the side, he snagged the box out of the sand. "This is for you."

Her fingers trembled a bit as she tugged the ring free. "It's beautiful."

His breath whooshed out in a relieved rush. "I'm glad you like it. You can't see it, but it's inscribed with our initials and the day we met. We'll add our wedding date to the inscription when we're married." He set the box down, took the ring from her, and slid it on her finger. "I love you, Whitney. You are the most amazing woman I've ever met. I can't wait to spend the rest of my life with you."

How could she not kiss him? She shifted on his lap until she straddled him, slid her arms around his neck, and melded her mouth with his. Their tongues twined, and the kiss was all lips and teeth and tongues, each of them struggling for control. He pulled her closer, plastering their bodies together. She felt the hard prodding of his cock between her thighs, and she moaned. Her pussy went slick in moments, already anticipating the thrust of his sex into hers. When his hand closed over her breast, her nipples beaded for him. She broke the kiss to let her head fall back, arching her torso into his hand.

"Ah, nice." He rubbed his thumb across one tight crest before he slipped his fingers under her bikini top to pinch a nipple. "So ready for me."

"Yes," she whispered, rolling her hips against his, simulating the erotic act she craved.

He groaned, his free hand clamping down on her ass to still her movements. "No more of that, honey, or I won't last."

She saw a flash of his white teeth in the moonlight, a truly wicked smile. "What?"

"Let's take a dip in the ocean."

The idea intrigued her. She'd never had sex underwater before, and definitely not in public. It shouldn't sound as enticing as it did. "I don't think we're supposed to swim at night."

The protest was weak and he knew it. His grin widened and he lifted her to her feet, leading her across the sand. "Who's watching?"

No one she cared about, and no one who'd be able to really tell what was going on in the dark. She squeezed his fingers and dashed into the water with him, wading out until they were chest-deep. She shivered as it chilled her. Then Drew yanked her into his arms and the water temperature didn't matter. His heat wrapped around her, and the waves swirled around them. She curved an arm around his shoulders to anchor herself and slid her other hand down his body, delving underneath the edge of his shorts and curling her fingers over his hard cock. Stroking the length of him, she felt an answering throb in her pussy. God, she wanted him inside her. Now. She pushed down his swim trunks until she freed his dick then continued to toy with his thick shaft.

He groaned softly, arching into her touch. His hands closed over her ass, lifting her off her feet so she was forced to wrap her legs around his trim waist. The water glued them together, and she felt the nudge of his cock against her lower belly. Tingles rippled down her skin, and her heart pounded in her chest. She writhed against him, craving more, needing that connection. Needing him.

"Damn, Whitney. I want to be inside you." He slipped his fingers down the curve of her ass until he could touch her from behind. Instead of stroking her slit, he jerked the inset of her bikini bottom aside, the head of his dick pressing for rough entrance. He hilted himself within her in one swift thrust. The stretch was divine, and her breath caught.

They moved together, the ocean roiling around them, the caress of the water somehow making the moment more erotic. His gripped her backside, holding her for his penetration. "I love the feel of you all tight and hot around me."

The words were an electric shock going through her pussy, and she clenched around him. They both groaned, but he kept his pace steady, pushing them closer to climax. It wouldn't be long before she came, and she threw herself toward the edge of oblivion. She wanted to share that bliss with him, now that they'd renewed their bond to each other. He moved one hand under her bikini bottom until he could tease the rim of her anus. Then he pushed into her there as well, filling her ass with his fingers. It was enough to send her flying. Orgasm ripped through her, and her pussy fisted around his cock. She opened her mouth on his shoulder, biting down to keep from crying out for anyone on the beach to hear.

He shuddered, his come pumping into her. "I love you, Whitney. Always."

"I love you," she echoed. "Always."

It might have had a shaky start, but she had a feeling this vacation was going to end up just as perfect as she'd hoped.

KISS OF PEACE

Dominic Santi

Sunday morning's 10:00 o'clock Mass was packed.

"Peace be with you," I murmured, leaning over to kiss Carli's warm, soft lips. I always gave my wife a kiss of peace first. I kissed each of our three fidgeting kids on the top of the head. Only then did I turn to shake hands with the other people around us.

I didn't care who knew how much I loved my family. They were the greatest gift God had ever given me. Carli and I had been married nine years. We had two boys, eight and six, who looked nothing like each other, despite how much they resembled various and sundry of my brothers' kids. Our two-year-old hellion was the mirror image of Carli's great-great-grandmother in the picture taken when the surviving members of the O'Neill clan disembarked at Ellis Island.

God, I loved them. My eyes filled and I quickly turned back toward the altar, tipping my head back and waiting for the burn of emotion to ease. Again. This had been happening way too much lately. I told myself I was just tired. I was almost thirty.

With the budget cuts, I'd been working lots of doubles. A fire-fighter's knees and back wear out fast.

Yesterday, I'd walked in the door after a twenty-four-hour shift to find my wife and kids wrapped together in a quilt on the couch, watching Saturday morning cartoons. Meggie sucked her thumb as she rested her face against Carli's breast. I told myself it was residual smoke from that last call that had my eyes filling. We'd fought a nasty warehouse fire for hours. Veterans like me were too tough to cry for no reason, especially when everybody else was laughing at the coyote chasing that stupid bird.

Firefighters weren't too tough to get an erection in church, though, especially when they were exhausted and horny. Remembering Carli on the couch had my cock filling. She'd been wearing the white silk nightgown and robe I'd gotten her for our last anniversary. It was low cut enough to show off a hint of her cleavage and complement her long black hair and bright blue eyes. With the robe's belt tightened, I couldn't see the shadows of her nipples. I couldn't rub my sooty, stubbled face against her breasts and suck her nipples to hard, wet peaks through just her nightgown's single layer of softly abrasive silk.

That had to wait for night and privacy, until the kids were finally asleep. Again. This morning, I held my hymnal firmly over my crotch, keeping a smile planted on my face and looking steadily up at the altar as the priest got ready for communion. No matter how much Carli said she liked seeing me in that damn gray wool suit, I should never have let her talk me into buying anything that showed off a hard-on the way those pants did. I wasn't surprised when she quietly slid her hand into mine and squeezed. A drop of precum leaked out of my cock, wetting the cotton of my briefs.

I knew better than to look at her, though. I was afraid she'd unconsciously do something like run her tongue over the edge of her lips, the way she'd done three months after we were married. I'd come in my pants, right there in the church. Thank god it had been winter then, too. I'd been able to slip my coat back on. As soon as Mass was over and we'd raced to the car, I'd started kissing her, ignoring the laughs and throat clearings outside as we'd steamed up the windows necking while the parking lot cleared.

I'd broken every speed record posted on the way home. We'd fucked on the couch inside the front door, our coats still on and my sticky pants around my ankles. Carli hiked her skirt up to her waist and threw her panties on the coffee table. I came so hard my teeth rattled—or maybe that was the lamp shaking when the couch banged against it.

Afterward, we figured if she was going to get pregnant that day, it was already too late. So we pulled off our clothes the rest of the way. We fucked on the couch again, then in the bed and in the shower, and after lunch, with her straddling me while I sat on her vanity chair. I hadn't thought I had another drop of cum in me. But she reached between us and guided the tip of my cock to her pussy lips. She slid slowly and sensuously down onto me, rocking back and forth with her nipples brushing against me. She cried out my name, over and over, her face flushed as she shook with orgasms. I cupped her bottom, thrusting up into her while her pussy sucked me off. I came so hard the room got fuzzy and I think I forgot to breathe.

Carli wrapped her arms and legs around me and buried her face in my neck. As her tears wet my skin, I felt the warm trickle of my semen running out of her and onto my balls. I loved her so much I was terrified, but I still held on to her tightly.

Micky was born nine months later, to the day, a fact that Carli's brother duly noted when I handed him a cigar, though he had the good sense to keep his mouth shut when Father Murphy asked him how he'd earned the honor of being godfather. I told Rob that since he'd been keeping track of his nephew for that long already, I figured he'd keep an eye on him for the long haul.

Our second son, Sean, had been planned. Carli and I made love almost every day for two months, trying to get her pregnant. I looked into her eyes while I climaxed and silently wondered which of the sperm exploding through my cock would eventually connect with her egg. Even now that Sean was six and learning to read, every time I thought about those days, every single time, I got hard remembering how incredible it had felt coming inside Carli while we made our second baby.

Meggie had been another surprise, though in retrospect, not that much of one. We hadn't been that concerned with consequences the week we'd left the boys with Carli's mother and slipped away for a marriage retreat. When Meggie was born, we were glad to have a daughter, and the boys were happy to have a sister to torment.

Nowadays, though, with three kids, a mortgage, and the kids' college funds having taken such a hit with the latest round of stock market upheavals, we couldn't afford to take those kinds of chances anymore. As I walked up to communion, I held my squirming daughter, thankful for the distraction as I offered up a prayer of thanks for my family, and for keeping my erection somewhat at bay as I dealt with our littlest handful. I figured God understood about the physical reactions that made me want my wife enough to make children with her. And since He gave her to me, I hoped He didn't mind that just thinking about her caused my body to show its appreciation, even when I was in church.

Today, my body was in overdrive showing appreciation. Carli and I were committed to using natural family planning. Not that

I wouldn't have broken all the rules if her life or health had been at stake. But they weren't. And though we'd love another baby if one came along, I didn't want to wear Carli out physically, the way both our mothers had been with so many pregnancies. Fortunately, Father Murphy's prenuptial classes had been embarrassingly explicit. When Micky was six months old, I'd bought our parish priest a beer down at the local pub to thank him for being so blunt.

Over the years, Carli and I had taken more classes. We'd prayed for guidance and strength. After a while I'd convinced myself I was a masochist to the core for coming to like the way we did things. Despite the blue balls and the wet dreams and occasionally succumbing to the temptation of letting Carli suck me off for the pure relief of it, I liked the desperate horniness of coming into her at the end of each month's abstinence.

When Carli wasn't fertile, we fucked like weasels. Two, three, four times a day, though now that I was getting older it had been a while since four had happened. Now, when she straddled me, it was usually on the bed, after she'd massaged my whole body with hers then sucked me until I was ready to explode.

Today, though, I couldn't have her. Carli was ovulating. If her temperature and the other indicators hadn't told us, the glow in her face would have been a dead giveaway. That, and the way she'd subconsciously squeezed her legs together when she leaned against the wall talking on the phone that morning, her nipples pebbling at the slight waft of cold air when the kids opened the front door. Carli got so horny when she was ovulating. I could smell her musk, even in church, even when I was corralling the kids and talking to the priest and it was totally inappropriate for me to be thinking how good my wife's pussy tasted. I couldn't wait for night to come. Maybe tonight I'd stay awake long enough to lick her until she screamed. I'd yet to find a serious

Biblical prohibition against eating my wife's pussy.

"Earth to Michael! May we take the kids to a movie today?"

Totally disoriented, I stared down into my mother's laughing face. She was waving her heavily ringed fingers in front of my nose. I stole a glance at Carli, who winked. My face heated at the sudden possibility of having my wife to myself all afternoon. Mom squeezed my arm.

"Carli says she doesn't mind, as long as Meggie gets her nap. So if you don't have any objections, we'll bring them back at dinnertime. Don, catch her please!"

"Yes, ma'am!" My dad laughed. He held out his arms and Meggie, squealing, detoured from trying to knock over a pile of church bulletins and let herself be hoisted into the air and twirled around. As the two of them waved and headed off toward the parking lot, I muttered, "Sure," and Mom gave me a meaningful look.

"You two need some time together. You work too hard— both of you." With a quick kiss to my cheek, she stepped back, then kissed Carli and strode off to help my dad collect the boys. Carli walked over and gave me a quick peck on the lips.

"She saw you looking at me, and she wants more grand-children, hot stuff." Carli rubbed subtly against me as people continued to flow out of the church and past us. I was instantly hard, and I knew she knew it, though I was horrified at the idea of my mother knowing what I was thinking. Carli laughed softly.

"Don't worry, she didn't say anything specific." Carli wrapped her arm around mine as she turned us toward the parking lot. "She and your dad just exchanged one of those looks—you know, the look that got you five brothers."

My face heated again as she surreptitiously pressed her breast against my forearm. Once more, I was thankful for my heavy winter coat. My cock couldn't decide if it wanted to deflate at the whole idea of my parents knowing how badly I wanted to have sex with my wife—and at the thought of how I'd gotten so many brothers—or if it wanted to get even harder remembering each of the times Carli had gotten pregnant. My hard-on won. As the wetness on my underwear pressed against my cock tip, though, I once more stopped and stepped back, this time to the edge of the sidewalk.

"Another baby?" I asked quietly. Part of me wanted to scream, yes, yes, YES! But a very loud voice that wasn't being governed by my throbbing cock was asking that question in a much more serious tone. Carli's eyes sparkled warmly as she reached up to rub her mittened hand over the side of my cheek.

"Part of me would love to have another baby with you, Michael," she said quietly, standing on tiptoe to kiss me. I held her closely, vaguely remembering that day so long ago when people had also been clearing their throats and laughing as they walked past us. But this time, Carli pulled back and stared seriously up into my eyes. "We've talked about this, though, when our libidos weren't screaming quite as loudly as they are right now. Is that really what we want to do?"

Carli's face was flushed with how turned on she was. My cock was so hard I hurt. But she was right. I shook my head, willing my cock to behave, trying to think about anything but how much I wanted my wife naked and reaching for me. I lost the battle when she leaned up and whispered in my ear.

"How about we go home and indulge in some good, hot 'alternative lovemaking' that won't get me pregnant? I want you to lick my pussy so bad."

Once more, I fought to keep from coming. I choked out, "Yes, ma'am!" and let her lead me to the car.

Carli drove. She said she figured I'd get a ticket. She was right. I would have figured it was worth it, even though by now, I knew all the cops in town, and I would have heard about it for nine months and then some afterward.

We took our coats off this time, but Carli and I still didn't make it upstairs. We had a bigger house now, two stories, and over the years we'd made love in every room. I kicked the front door closed and threw my coat on the thickly carpeted steps. Then I stripped my wife naked, kissing my way down her neck and shoulders as I slowly unzipped her dress and pulled it down to her waist. I slid the top of her slip down and lapped across the tops of her breasts, dampening the lacy cups covering her hard nipples. She sighed contentedly when I released the catch of her bra. Her breasts fell warm and heavy into my hands. Her nipples were larger and darker now, the tips longer and so much more sensitive on my tongue than they had been before the babies.

"Harder," she whispered, wrapping her arms around my head as she stepped out of her shoes. She moved up onto the stairs, her feet sliding on the satin lining of my coat as she situated herself so I wouldn't have to bend my neck. "That feels so good, Mike. It makes me so hot." She pressed her chest to my face, moaning as I licked slowly over to the other breast and sucked the whole areola into my mouth.

Her groan of pleasure had my cock ready to split my pants. I suckled one side, then the other, back and forth, smiling as she held my head ferociously to her. I slowly worked her dress and slip over her hips. She was wearing lace-topped, thigh-high stockings rather than panty hose. I hadn't thought my cock could get harder, but it did as I peeled her panties from her hips and let them drop over the lacy bands.

"You'll have to lie down for me to get your stockings off,"

I growled against her, nipping her swollen nipple as I ran my hands down her silky thighs.

"You're pretty overdressed, yourself, pal." She arched an eyebrow at me when I shook my head.

"If I take my pants off now, you're going to get pregnant," I said, my chest heaving as my cock strained against my pants. I eased her down onto my overcoat. "Spread your legs and come for me, woman. I want to feel you orgasm under my tongue."

Carli leaned back on the stairs, giving me a sultry look as she opened her legs wide. She grabbed a rung of the banister in one hand. With the other hand, she rubbed her pussy. Her dark pubic hair glistened with her juices. She touched her finger to the apex of her slit and shivered hard.

"Put your tongue on my pussy, Michael. I want you to lick me—right here."

With a loud groan, I sank to the stairs and lowered my head between her thighs. Carli knew how much her talking dirty turned me on. Her musk filled my nostrils as I nuzzled her slippery pussy lips. I licked her juices from her while Carli leaned back against the stairs, her fingers sliding from her crotch to dig into the carpet. She moaned and raised her legs. I turned my head and kissed her thigh, peeling a stocking off and dropping it onto the floor. Then I took the other one off.

"I don't want you wearing anything but your wedding rings," I growled, feasting my eyes on the sight of her flushed, curvy body. Her eyes glowed. Her well-sucked nipples perked up wet and dark and hard. Her glistening pussy quivered, waiting for me to eat her into ecstasy. I sank down onto the staircase, my cock once again pressing desperately into my precum-wet briefs and the edge of the stair. I lifted her thighs to my shoulders and spread her legs as wide as I could. Then I buried my face in my wife's pussy and commenced to eating her to my heart's content.

It felt good to be able to be loud. I growled and demanded, slurping as I told Carli in graphic detail the things I usually had to whisper, how I loved the smell and taste of her pussy, how I loved licking inside her to slurp her slippery juices, that I knew they were flowing to ease the way for my cock, even though today she was only going to get my tongue and fingers. I flicked the little nub that made her shake and cry out, licking until my tongue was almost numb, then panting against her as my fingers, two and then three and then four, pressed deep into her, rubbing up toward her belly button. Shortly after Sean was born, Carli had stunned me by blushingly admitting that sometimes, if I pressed just right, she came so hard she could feel her juice shooting out. Once I'd learned where to press, I'd also learned how to position myself so her clear, slippery juice squirted onto my face.

"Mike!" Carli gasped, arching up so hard she banged her pubic bone on my face. "Yes! Oh, god! I'm going to come!"

Carli stiffened, keening as the tremors began deep inside her. Grinning, I lowered my head again, flailing her clit as she bucked up, her pussy muscles tightening almost painfully against my hand. She screamed and I sucked her clit into my mouth, still flicking mercilessly as I ground my cock against the carpeting and pressed my fingers up harder inside her. As the next scream left her lips, her juices spurted onto my chin.

I came in my pants. I rocked helplessly against the stairs, sucking Carli's clit and fucking her with my fingers until she finally pushed my face away. I kept my fingers in her though, pressing and rocking until she groaned and quivered again, her pussy once more spasming quietly over my hand. She tenderly pulled me up to her and kissed my face until I tasted her juices on her tongue.

We left my coat and her clothes on the stairs as we shakily

took each other's hands and stumbled into the bedroom. Carli peeled my shirt and socks and my cum-soaked pants from me, laughing as she kissed the tip of my now-quiescent shaft and drew me down onto the sheets with her. I barely remember her pulling the covers over us. I slept like a rock. When we finally woke up, the sun was low in the afternoon sky. We cuddled and talked and laughed. I ate her pussy and she sucked my cock, not enough to get off again, but enough to feel really good and let us both know how hungry we'd be for each other all over again when this month's fertile cycle had passed. There was just enough time to take a shower and get our clothes off the stairs before the kids came home.

My parents will be disappointed when there's no baby nine months from now. And like I said, if there's an accident some-where down the line, they'll have another name to list in the family Bible, with no regrets on our part. No matter what happens, though, I know the passion I share with Carli is the greatest blessing I'll ever have on earth. I intend to keep nurturing that passion. And if that means I have to deal with hard-ons in church, well, so be it. God gave me Carli to love. I figure He'll understand.

GROUNDED

Nikki Magennis

Erin arrived first. Her red-eye flight landed hard and ground to a slow halt. She stepped out onto a flat gray desert of tarmac. The air was twelve degrees colder and everything was quiet, the airport still half asleep. Inside the terminal, Erin stashed her case in a locker and then walked circuits round empty lounges and past shuttered shops, trying to work the stiffness out of her legs. It was like wandering in Limbo. A space between destinations, a no-man's-land. Airports seemed to exist outside of any particular place, but she loved them, felt at ease in their anonymous spaces, unknown and free. Foreign voices echoed around her, as hushed as pigeons' wings.

She bought breakfast, a cinnamon wafer and hot, strong coffee, but her appetite dissolved, replaced by a swarm of butterflies in her stomach. Instead, she went to the newsstand and flicked through magazines on the carousel, looking at pictures until the colors blurred: a face painted blue, a crowd at a race, a map of Europe dotted with flags.

An hour later she watched from behind the plate glass windows as Mark's flight landed. It was like watching silent movie footage on a vast, blue-tinted screen. He emerged from the plane into the Dutch morning light. The sight of him, six foot, tanned, lithe and weather-roughed made her heart beat double-espresso fast. She got a glimpse of his two-day stubble and crumpled clothes before he disappeared into the walkway, swallowed by another passage, gone from her again.

She found herself finger-combing her hair and biting her lip, like a teenager.

"Erin." His smile was as wide as a sunrise. They crossed the last distance separating them like they were drawn by gravity, and sank into an embrace so tight she could hardly breathe. She pressed her face into the coarse, air-cold folds of his jacket, inhaled all the smells that made her heart ache. Woodsmoke, cut grass, pine. He smelled like spring.

"God, I missed you," he said, talking into her hair, his words warm against her scalp. At the sound of his voice she felt her eyes prickle.

"Me, too," she said.

"Oh, babe. Where have you been?"

"All over the place," she said. There was so much to say, but then he held her chin and lifted her face to kiss her and it was clear they needed to touch more than they needed to speak. He tasted sweet. His body was hard and insistent against hers. His arms locked around her and held her tight.

She pulled away, looked around and saw where they were, on a polished floor, in the stream of traffic, taking up space. They'd hardly touched each other but she already felt like she was naked. She coughed.

"Got a bag?" she asked, her voice a breaking whisper. Did the question even make sense? She was fixed on his eyes, their blue gaze still shocking bright behind half-closed lids. He shrugged one shoulder.

"Just this."

"C'mon." Her mouth was thick from kissing him. The words bumped against one another. Now, they laced their fingers together and walked over the squeaky, shined floors, past the fragmented groups of people wandering, dazed and sleep scuffed, around the airport, weaving between knots of Japanese tourists, struggling families, scowling businessmen, cabin crew in their bright, tired uniforms, under signs and hanging curtains of LEDs and scrolling announcement boards and arrows pointing in so many different directions. His thumb brushed the pulse spot on her wrist, and it seemed to turn up the volume of her heartbeat. The ambient sounds faded, her pulse became as loud as their footsteps, louder than all the things she wanted to say but couldn't and didn't know how to phrase anyway, until it drummed in her head and all she could think of was his bare skin against hers.

They reached the doorway of the pod hotel where she'd booked a room. "Give me a minute," she said, pulling out her credit card and trying to find the right slot to swipe it in the check-in machine. Her hands were shaking. Behind her, Mark came up and rested his chin on her shoulder.

"Stop."

"Hmm? I'm not doing anything," he said, scuffing her neck with the rough scrape of his stubble. Her knees almost buckled and she leaned against the machine with both hands flat on the screen. He laid a tiny, wet kiss on her hairline and she closed her eyes.

"I can't work the thing. Come on."

"I've waited six weeks," he said, his voice so low it sunk into the carpet. "Okay. Do it. Get us in there. I need you in a room, naked, now." He backed away, holding his hands up, and she instantly missed the feel of him next to her.

"Don't go anywhere," she said. She typed in her number and got the key. They followed arrows, counting cabin numbers along the corridors, trying not to paw at each other, almost succeeding.

"In here," she said, tugging him through a narrow doorway and pulling the door shut behind them. The space was so small a few lungs full of breath would fill it. Against the spotless white walls of the cabin he was so vivid. So real and so close. At last she could inhale him and touch him and feel the different textures of him—his soft hair; the heat of his skin; his wet, hungry mouth.

She looped her arms round his neck and sagged against him, but he pulled away, placed a hand on her chest.

"Wait."

"More?" she almost laughed, but it caught in her throat. "Fuck, Mark."

He wasn't smiling.

"I've got something in mind." He slipped his rucksack off his back and pushed into her hands. "Open it."

Erin frowned. She didn't want gifts. They'd agreed. She had to travel light. "What is this?"

Mark stayed silent. She shook her head and unzipped the bag. Reaching inside, her hand met something cool and silk slippery. Rope. She pulled out a length of long, black cord, wrapped around her hand like a waiting snake.

"Mark?" She looked inside the bag. At the bottom was a box of condoms and a small tube of lube. Nothing else.

She paused. She wanted to smile but her mouth wouldn't cooperate. Her hands swarmed with the need for him. "Drop it on the bed," Mark said, indicating the rope. She did as he asked.

"I'm going to undress you," he said, moving toward her and

tugging at her buttons. Somehow, she was rooted to the spot. "Let me." He undid her steadily, tugging her arms free and throwing her jacket on the floor as if it was dirty laundry. "Good," he nodded, at her mute assent. Now he gripped her arms.

"If you want me to stop say so, okay?"

She opened her mouth but nothing came out. She nodded.

He continued to strip her: shirt, vest, chinos, roughly peeled off and discarded. Erin felt like her breath was too loud. She wanted to swallow but somehow felt embarrassed. "Mark," she said at last, "please kiss me."

He laughed.

"It's been so long. This isn't fair."

"Really? You ought to be used to going without. Told me to enjoy the anticipation, remember?"

Erin moaned. "You're punishing me."

"Not yet." Now he unbuttoned the top of his jeans. His cock sprang from his fly, thick and stiff. Then he pulled his shirt over his head, and she got a face full of his scent—shower gel spice tinged with fresh sweat. He was beautiful. She hadn't forgotten, but the sight still left her reeling: his work-taut body, always restless, always in motion. The drift of black hair that clung to his chest and crept down his stomach, spreading as it disappeared into his jeans. And his coolness, his ease in his own skin. Nothing ever seemed to faze him. As he came up hands-reach close only a twitch of his pretty red lips showed any reaction to her proximity, or her near nakedness.

He lifted the rope and wound it around his hands. "Now, let me fix you."

He pulled her wrists behind her. The subtle pulse that beat between her legs intensified. Every muscle in her legs threatened to turn liquid, and she wondered how long she could hold herself up. The slight touch of his fingers as he secured her and checked the knots was like fine sandpaper. When the edge of his fingernail caught slightly against her hip it stung like she'd been lashed. Not painful, but a bright, dizzying burn, as if her desire was concentrated and written into that one thin dash.

"I'm going to fuck you so hard," he said, his mouth up close to her ear and so quiet she hardly heard it. But she did. Her body heard it. His words struck deep in her center, and her spine curled.

"Okay," she said, "Mark, please."

She held herself tensed and steady, trying not to rock back and forth. She'd wanted him for so long, his voice and hands and mouth and cock. The memory of how good he felt and how tightly they fit together had been reignited with every phone call, every text and blurry phone video. Standing in the shade of a tall plane tree in Tunis, she'd filled a phone with dull brassy coins and stood listening to the unfamiliar dial tone, each unanswered beep like a castigation, a lament for traveling so far, for being elsewhere; a way of noting the uncountable miles that separated her from her lover.

Now, in this antiseptic little cabin, with the anonymous sheets and the empty corridors, with the endless flow of millions of strangers around them and the thought of how many others had used this room, used this bed, her heart started to ache like it might burst.

"I want you," she said at last, splaying her hands against each other, feeling the chill of the air-con roughen her skin with goose bumps, seeing the faint smudge of Mark's reflection in the shower glass and thinking how she so rarely got more than a brief taste, a furious, hurried embrace.

"Yep," Mark said, as if he was hardly listening. He looked her over, thoughtfully. Then he pulled the chair in close and turned it toward her.

"Sit," he said, tipping his head at the seat. Startled, she obeyed without thinking, and landed with a jolt. Now, he took another length of cord from the rucksack and crouched down, patting Erin's calf. "Shift your feet." He wrapped first one ankle, then the other, fastening them to the cold metal of the chair legs. Erin sat with her legs spread, feeling more exposed as her ability to move was gradually restricted. Mark worked quietly, as calm as if he were fixing a tarp to a trailer.

When he was finished, he dropped his hands to his thigh and looked her over. "Test them," he said. Erin's eyes widened. She wasn't used to instructions from him—this was her warm, kind, laughing Mark, all business. There was flint in his gaze, an unsettling purposefulness in his movements. His want reached her as a force, so strong that it couldn't be deflected. Her hips had started to ache from being spread. Was he testing her? Trying to trick her into giving up control?

"Okay," she nodded. "I'll play."

She pulled against her ties to see how far she could move. Not far. The ropes were soft, twisted cotton, and the memory of where she'd felt them before came back to her. Lead ropes. For horses. She pictured Mark walking across the back fields, the rope running through his hands and the dew wetting his boots.

"What are you smiling at?" he asked, lifting his eyes to her face.

"Nothing," she said, "it's good to see you."

"You like that, huh?"

She shrugged, or tried to. "Not what I was expecting."

"Hmm." He leaned forward and nuzzled at the lace edge of her bra, finding her nipple and catching it in his teeth.

"Ah."

He bit gently, until she cried out again, then nipped at the other one. His mouth left wet patches. "I could eat you up," he said, the burr of his accent softened by a whisper but still slanted with the Island accent she used to tease him about.

He gripped her waist, now, with both hands. He worked at her, kneading her flesh, rubbing down to her splayed thighs and pressing into the tender skin there. She could feel the heat of his breath against her belly and it made her want to twitch.

"Mark."

His thumbs hooked under her knickers and tugged the elastic away from her body. She felt the air-conditioned air on her, heard nothing but the motionless air in the tiny space, slowly heating up and growing closer. Usually she got claustrophobic pretty quickly. Right now she wanted the walls to close in farther, to squeeze against her. The desire contained in her was turning almost violent, the immobility wildly frustrating. Waves inside her pulsed from her belly to her cunt and back again. She struggled in her seat. The tightness of her bonds was good. She fought against the rope, confident she would lose.

"You look good like that," he said, sitting back and leaving her with her pants half pulled down her thighs, squirming in her seat. He wet his lips with the tip of his tongue. She stared at his mouth, mesmerized.

"Don't make me beg you," she said, her voice cut back to a whisper.

"I won't make you do anything you don't want to do, you know that, babe," he said, a familiar, lazy smile hovering over his mouth.

Erin tilted her hips, trying to twist and press herself against the seat.

"Poor girl. You're in need," he said, dropping his gaze to her lap. "How long's it been?"

Erin shook her head. Her cheeks were flushed and her breath was ragged.

"Answer the question. How long?"

"We saw each other in…April? Six weeks."

"Did you miss me?"

"You know I did."

"Answer the question." He reached out and pulled at her knickers, tugging the elastic against the back of her thighs so it dug lines into her skin.

"Yes. I missed you." Erin blushed harder.

"Did you fuck anyone else?"

"Mark. Of course not."

"Did you want to?"

They looked at each other. "I don't play jealous games, Mark."

"Who said I was jealous? I just want to know."

"I was working, for fuck's sake. Sweating my way round the Sahara. Sleeping in trucks, sometimes. No, I didn't want anyone else."

She looked away, biting her lip.

"Good." He slid one fingertip inside her, cool and gentle. Curled his hand against her, covering her pussy with his palm and a warm, maddeningly soft touch. She gasped. So slight. Her muscles tried to tighten around him.

"Not yet," he said. She pressed her mouth closed. Held still and took a deep breath.

"More." She kept her voice steady. "Please. Give me more."

"Funny. That's just what I was going to ask next." Mark leaned in close, so she could smell his hair. Mint and seaweed.

"See, I've been waiting, too. It's taken me a long while to realize. I spoke to you last week, remember?"

Erin nodded, trying to concentrate on his words instead of his fingers.

"And you were talking about the fixer and complaining

about the coffee and the heat and it hit me."

"What?"

He looked at her full in the face. "You're never coming home, are you?"

Erin shook her head. "Don't do this now."

"We only have now, Erin."

"And you want to know if I'm coming home? I don't have an answer. I don't even know what that word means anymore. Probably not the same as it does to you. The valley. The farm. But you won't leave, will you?"

"Leave my work? Let my parents struggle on without me? No. That's not possible."

Erin threw her head back and squeezed her eyes shut.

"Mark, *we* are not possible. We're the impossible couple. We always come back to this. But here we are. Let's talk about this later." She sighed. "I just want to touch you. Kiss me. Please."

"You know how much I want to," he said. "But this time, not without a promise."

"Don't do it. Don't you dare."

"What, ask you to give it up? Oh, I'd love it. For you to turn up at the farm in the breaking dawn one morning and climb into my bed and tell me you're never going to leave. We could just sink into each other." He worked at her now, slowly, his fingers describing a delicate curve over her clit before pinching her, hard enough for her eyes to widen.

"Take our time. See where we got to." He slid his fingers inside her again, worked at the sweet spot.

Erin closed her eyes. "There. There is good."

"That's what I thought. Here. Here is good. You know why?"

"Hmm."

"Believe it or not, a shoebox hotel room buried on the

outskirts of Amsterdam is not my dream destination."

"It was the best we could do. Next time we'll make it some-where sexier."

"Next time it's harvest, Erin, next time it's lambing. Next time I won't have any weekends left. But it doesn't matter."

"'Course it does. But so does kissing me."

"Just stop for a minute." He pulled away suddenly, and Erin gave a sharp intake of breath. "Listen." He turned and rifled in his jean pockets, pulled out a condom and tore it open. He kept talking as he unrolled the rubber onto his cock.

"Here is good because a six-thirty flight from Tunis can get you to within touching distance of a two-hour flight from Aber-deen. Here is good because you are here and that's the only place I really want to be."

As he talked, he maneuvered himself so that the tip of his cock was pointed directly at her crotch.

"With you." He buried a hand in her hair. "In you."

"Yes." She spoke without thinking, and he entered her at the same time, sliding inside in one movement, meeting the resis-tance and overcoming it until he was as deep as he could go. Erin opened her mouth but made no sound at all. She fought to inhale. As he started to pull back and fuck her rhythmically, slowly but decisively, the cabin filled with the sound of their scorched breath.

With one hand still holding a handful of her hair, he held her in position. Although she wanted to rub against him, to push all the burning points of her body at the taut, hard surfaces of his, Erin could only twist in her ropes. The plastic chair was slippery and her skin stuck to it.

"Please," she said, willing him for more. They were fixed together on his terms, his tempo, and there was nothing she could do about it. The imbalance made her want to scream, but then she looked at his face, the curve of his cheekbone and his slightly open mouth, the taut muscle of his arm as he tensed in position. His eyes stuck on hers. For once, she held still.

"Yes," she said, and gave in. At once her body brimmed with sensation. Pleasure flooded through her, sweet and hopeless. He fucked her faster and she could have cried with gratitude.

When his fingers slid between them and pinched at her clit, she ground her teeth together. Now they were tangled so thick and deep she felt the buildup start. It had the same force as a plane bowling down a runway. The sensation of irresistible pressure overtook her, and they were no longer just two bodies writhing together, no longer all clit and cock and cunt. He pressed hard against her, rough and desperate, fucking her with his teeth gritted, and then he was still. She called his name. As in a lucid dream, she sensed the ground fall away, and they were suddenly weightless.

The moment of lightness, then, as always, was shocking in its impossibility. It lifted her into another place, somewhere wordless and free. As Mark came inside her, she rested her cheek on his shoulder and felt the orgasm shake through her body and echo in his. He gave a low gasp. For a minute or two they stayed like that, drifting.

They laughed as they broke apart, Mark unfolding himself slowly, bumping against the furniture.

"What was the promise?" Erin asked. "I'd say yes to anything right now."

"Thank god for that."

Erin opened her eyes. Mark was kneeling in front of her, hunching his hands into his pockets. He held out his hand, palm up. A ring. A bright, glittering stone.

It was just a circle of metal and a piece of pretty rock. It couldn't weigh more than a few grams. Maybe it was just the unexpectedness of it that made her want to cry. Erin felt all the swimming emotion go out of her, flow down her arms and legs and center on this brilliant point of light.

She wanted to reach out then, but the ropes held her steady. Suddenly she needed to be out, to be free. She tensed against the bindings.

"Mark, let me go now."

He looked up. "If that's what you want."

Erin's belly flipped as if she'd just hit a pocket of turbulence. "I don't mean us," she said, throwing a nod behind her. "I mean this, these knots."

"I do mean us," Mark said softly. "If you want, I'll let you go. Otherwise, take the ring. I don't care where you are, Erin. If you'll wear this, I'll know you'll come home again."

She looked up. Her voice was soft. "I don't know how we can make it work."

"Are you saying no?"

Outside, a group of women made their way noisily along the corridor, tried the door handle. "Sorry," someone shouted, and someone else laughed.

Erin shook her head.

"I'm saying I don't know if I can give you what you want."

Mark's hand closed shut. Erin stared at his curled fingers. "I don't want to lose you," she said at last. "But I know I can't ask you to wait for me."

She looked up. Mark's long, lazy smile was working its way onto his mouth. His eyes were sky blue, she thought, suddenly. How had she never noticed that before?

"Well, you know, I wouldn't be spending my whole time writing poetry on a lonely hillock in the rain. I might be able to function without you for—how long is the longest we've gone?"

"Twelve. Twelve weeks."

"Yeah. Given emails and a couple of naked video calls."

Erin bit back her own smile. "And what then?"

"Did I say I was psychic? I said I was in love with you."

"No you didn't. You said—"

"Don't split hairs, smart-ass. He took her chin in his hand and held her face steady. "I don't know what next. I don't know where or how. I just know who. We'll work the rest out. Don't you think?"

Erin smiled.

"Is that a yes? A yes for the moment? A yes and we'll see?"

"It's a yes. A yes, please. On one condition."

"Name it."

"Next time we're going to have a serious discussion, you're the one tied to a chair."

She darted forward and caught his mouth. He looped his arms around her back, loosed the knot at her wrists and untied her while he kissed her. They both closed their eyes and for a while, forgot where they were altogether.

SWEET MEMORIES

Kristina Wright

I turned the shower up as hot as it would go, rolling my aching shoulders under the spray. If anyone had asked, I would have said I wasn't thinking about anything except my five-year-old Garrett's birthday party. It was that afternoon at the park near our house and I had thirty guests coming, half of them kids, and the clouds were threatening rain. I was working out the details in my head, running my fingers through my tangled hair as I applied shampoo, then conditioner. And then, I was crying. Not just crying, sobbing. Great wracking sobs that echoed off the shower walls. Thankfully, the boys were at my mother's house and Brett was—well, that just made me sob some more. I thought Brett was picking up the birthday cake and the deli and fruit trays I'd ordered, but I couldn't be sure where he was. Not really. I couldn't be sure of anything anymore. Of course, neither could he.

It's funny what you remember over the course of a relationship. What lingers and what falls away. What seems important in the midst of a fight and what seems trivial when you're lying in each other's arms after three sweaty hours of lovemaking. When you sit back and inventory the moments, put them in plus and minus columns and look at the bottom line—what's left? Is it a bucket full of regrets and heartache, or is it a flood of sweet memories?

Sometimes it's both.

Sometimes, the happily ever after comes with a heaping helping of hurt and heartache. Sometimes, once you're gone, out of the relationship and moving on, you look back and wish for a do over. You can't go back, of course, and you can't do it over. It doesn't work that way. But sometimes you take a chance anyway and throw caution to the wind, knowing you're going to get hurt—and it's going to hurt like hell, just like it used to—but knowing the good times will be the best you ever had. Sometimes we take the pain for the chance at pleasure. Sometimes the pain *is* pleasure.

Books and movies rarely ever get it right. Oh, sure, they show the push-and-pull of a new relationship, the getting to know you, the misunderstandings. Sometimes they show the moment of reckless infidelity or casual cruelty that leads to the breakup—it's not a very good book or movie if there's no conflict, right?—but within fifty pages or twenty minutes, it's all resolved. Neatly, completely, and everyone lives happily ever after. The book ends, the movie fades to black and they never show you what happens after. After the hurt and the heartache, after the reconciliation.

And that's where I was. Where *we* were, Brett and me. There in that place of reconciliation. Of apologies and forgiveness, of insecurities and doubts, of tender, barely scabbed wounds still being nursed while we raised our two kids and shared the same house, if not the same bed. It had started with a drunken threesome gone awry—he spun it off into a twosome on nights he supposedly worked late and then I found my own hot, young cowboy to go two-stepping with on weekends when Brett took the boys camping or fishing. I think we both knew what was going on and didn't care. For a little while, I think we were even happy with the setup, though neither of us was open minded enough to broach it. Our own sex life ramped up in a way it hadn't since before our oldest, already seven years old, was born. Having our cake and eating it, too? Yeah, we gorged on cake and it made us both sick.

Six months after his coworker girlfriend transferred to a new department because she couldn't have him full-time and my cowboy rode off into the sunset with one of the bartenders who worked at the club where we liked to go dancing, Brett and I were still trying to figure out who we were to each other. We weren't what we had been in college, or as newlyweds or even as new parents. We were something different now. Something undefined. It left me feeling like my world wasn't quite in order. Like I wasn't quite myself now that there was a fissure in my most intimate relationship.

He was sleeping in the guest room. His choice. I offered, but he insisted. He's a gentleman like that and knows I prefer the comfort of my own bed. (Never mind the snide cracks made in heated arguments about whose bed I really preferred.) If not for the reason, I wouldn't have minded sleeping alone. It was nice having the big bed to myself, to have my space, to feel like I was living in my own skin if only for those few restless hours in bed, instead of being wife, mother, daughter, girlfriend and having all those people pulling at me, demanding things of me. But of course, Brett's absence from our bed—the first time we'd not slept in the same bed in our twelve years of marriage— was a constant reminder of what I'd done. What he'd done. What we had done to each other.

My sobs washed away with the hot water until I was shivering, my skin turning blue with goose bumps. I fumbled for the towel on the rack outside the shower and wrapped it around myself. Stepping out of the shower was like climbing out of my own thoughts and back into the real world. Neither was particularly comforting right now, but at least the real world offered distractions. And the boys. Thank god for Garrett and Douglas and their sweet, sticky faces. I'd have lost my mind by now if not for them—and I wondered if Brett and I would even still be married if not for the kids.

I could feel a fresh bout of tears building behind my eyelids, so I pushed the thought away and focused on the tasks at hand as I wrapped a towel around me. The cooler needed to be filled with ice, Garrett's presents had to be loaded in the car, I probably needed to grab a couple rolls of paper towels to go along with Transformers napkins, which were colorful but worthless against the mess-making capabilities of a pack of five-year-olds.

I walked to the kitchen, naked except for the towel, wet hair still dripping down my back, to make a list before I forgot the dozen last-minute details rattling around in my brain. I was so intent on not forgetting anything that I didn't hear the back door open until Brett's startled, "Oh!" pulled me out of my party-planning reverie.

I spun around and stared at him, feeling as startled as he looked. He had a cake box in one hand and two stacked deli trays in the other. I covered the awkwardness of the moment by hustling over to take the trays out of his hand.

"Hey," I muttered, keeping a tight grip on my towel with one hand while I settled the trays on the already crowded countertop. "I didn't hear you come in."

"Apparently."

"So, uh, the cake came out okay?"

I blushed at the stammer in my voice. This wasn't some stranger, this was my husband. He'd seen me naked. Hell, he'd seen me give birth—twice. There was no reason to feel uncomfortable or shy. And yet, I shifted from foot to foot, conscious of how short my towel was and how it gapped open high on my thigh as I moved.

"Take a look," he said, pulling the lid back to let me see it.

It was bright—primary colors and little toy robots and about a mountain of buttercream frosting. Garrett was going to love it. So would Douglas. So would the rest of the kids.

And—boom—I was crying again. I wouldn't have thought I had anything left in me, but fat tears were rolling down my cheeks. I turned away and leaned against the counter.

I heard Brett move behind me, shifting the trays on the counter to make way for the cake box. "What's wrong? I thought it looked okay."

He was either making a joke or he was too dense for words. I had known him long enough to know he wasn't dense. I attempted to laugh, but it was a hoarse bark. "It's great. Garrett will love it. Maybe it'll make up for his parents tiptoeing around the house like they're walking on eggshells."

He didn't respond. He didn't have to. That, at least, was something we could agree on.

I felt his presence behind me a moment before he wrapped his arms around my waist. It wasn't as if we hadn't touched in the past six months—we made a special show of being affectionate in front of the boys, as if that would erase the tension in their young lives. Behind closed doors, we gave each other a wide berth, as if touching privately, for real, was forbidden. But now, with his chin resting on my shoulder and his arms tight around my waist, I felt like it was the first time we'd ever touched.

But I wasn't touching him. My hands were on the counter, my

feet planted apart like I was going to attack anything in front of me. I tried to relax, dropped my arms at my sides and sunk into his embrace, but that didn't feel right either. I rested my hands on his forearms and leaned my head back against his chest.

"What are we doing?" he murmured against my ear. "What the *hell* are we doing?"

"We're being parents. We're taking care of our kids. We're being partners. We're trying to work things out."

"Work things out," he said the words as if they left a bad taste in his mouth. "It shouldn't be work. Love shouldn't be work."

I tensed, my heart hammering in my chest, the tears still streaming down my face. "This is a very, very bad time to tell me you're leaving me," I said in a small, tight voice.

I felt him shake his head. "Damn it, Carolyn, that's not what I'm saying at all. I'm saying it's not work to love you, it's not work to be with you, it's not work at all. We hit a speed bump, we can get over it."

I laughed. Leave it to Brett to minimize it. "Speed bump? That's how you see it?"

"How do you see it?"

"Tsunami," I said without pause, because I'd given it a lot of thought on all the lonely nights in our big bed. "Unexpected, out of the blue, complete devastation. End game."

"But it wasn't that at all. The warning signs were there all along and we are *not* devastated. We are not over."

Brett and I could argue over the color of the sky, that's the kind of relationship we had. In the end, we'd agree that it was some kind of blue. And in the end of this, we'd agree it was some kind of bad. We just had to sort it out, however long it took. I sighed.

He shifted behind me, his arms tightening. "I want you," he said.

I had been studiously trying to ignore the erection pressing against my terry-cloth covered ass. "No kidding?"

"No kidding."

I could've said no. I had a dozen reasons why we couldn't—shouldn't—have sex right then. Not the least of which was the birthday party that was starting in less than two hours. A crack of thunder reminded me that we might very well be hosting this party at our house if the weather didn't cooperate. So there were all kinds of reasons to pull away, walk away, get dressed and pretend like we hadn't just had the first real moment we'd shared in months.

Of course, I've never been one to walk away.

"Yes," I said simply, knowing he would understand my meaning.

He moved his hands up to my chest, undoing my towel with a flick of his thumb. The towel fell, his hands cupped my breasts and I pressed back against him, enjoying the hardness against me instead of feeling as if I had to ignore it.

A soft moan-sigh escaped me, and was answered by the press of his body against mine and his thumbs working their magic against my nipples.

"Yes," he murmured, licking the shell of my ear. "That's all, just yes? I was hoping for a little more enthusiasm."

He was teasing me. After everything we'd been through, he could still lighten the moment by teasing me. I laughed, feeling like something inside of me was loosening, cracking open, releasing me from my self-made prison. I swiveled my hips so that the towel slipped the rest of the way from my body and then I wriggled my ass against his crotch.

"Is that enthusiastic enough for you?"

"Getting there," he said, his hands gliding down the swell of my breasts to the indent of my waist before settling on my hips.

He pulled me back against him, firmly, determinedly, grinding his cock against my naked bottom.

"Here or—" I started to say, before he spun me around. I squealed in surprise as he picked me up and sat me on the edge of the counter.

"Here. No time like the present, no place better than here."

That's the thing about Brett. He's quick to make decisions and once he does—well, he can convince you he's made the absolute best decision. And as he planted his big hands on my thighs and spread them open, I absolutely believed he was right. Then he lowered his head between my legs and gave my bare and quickly moistening pussy a long, slow swipe with his tongue and there was no doubt in my mind that *now* and *here* were exactly right.

I braced my hands on the counter and leaned back, careful to avoid the party clutter, and closed my eyes as his mouth slowly devoured me. It had been so long—*too* long—since I'd had this kind of attention that it didn't take more than a few focused licks and my clit was throbbing. I wriggled on the counter, my juices making a slick spot beneath me, trying to focus his tongue where I wanted it. He was teasing me again, licking and sucking my labia, teasing my opening, fluttering his tongue against my clit, taking me to the cusp of orgasm, but making sure he never lingered long enough to let me go all the way.

Finally, when I couldn't take it any longer, I made a noise that sounded like a growl and reached down to grab his head between my thighs and pull it up close and tight to the very spot I needed him to lick. His tongue flattened out against my clit as I ground my crotch against his mouth. One, two, three, and I was coming, sliding to the edge of the counter so that the only thing keeping me from hitting the floor was his head nestled in the V of my spread legs. I thrust against his mouth, utterly shameless, intent on making my orgasm last as long as I could. As long as he could.

Brett didn't seem to mind that I was smothering him between my legs. His mouth pressed against me, licking and sucking my clit as I came. I could hear sounds of muffled appreciation as I coated his face with my juices. The smell of my arousal was thick and heavy in the air, but I felt light—as if a weight had been lifted from my chest, my heart. I laughed as his tongue kept nursing at my clit, the muscles in my thighs jumping as my oversensitive flesh protested the continuing onslaught. I pushed his head away, gasping and laughing and wriggling. He stood, catching me as I slid off the edge of the counter, and his cock was already out and hard, sliding into me as easily as a knife in a sheath. My gasp turned to a moan as he filled my wet pussy, still tight and pulsing from my orgasm.

"Yeah, baby," he whispered, hauling my legs up around his waist so that my weight was supported by his hands cupping my ass. "I've missed you."

We stood there like that for a long moment, my arms and legs wrapped tight around him, his cock buried so far inside of me that it almost hurt, our breathing synchronized, our faces so close that he looked blurry.

"I will always love you," he said. "Always. Nothing, no one can change that."

He thrust into me then, as if to emphasize his point. I gasped. I hitched my legs up higher on his waist, holding tighter, my body damp with sweat. I nuzzled his neck, licking along his jawline and the throb of the vein pulsing there.

"Nothing can break us," I whispered, knowing it to be true. Knowing it all along, but so hurt and sad that I couldn't see it. Couldn't feel it because I'd built such a wall of protection around me, to match the one he'd built for himself. But all the walls were down now. It was just the two of us, naked and vulnerable.

"Nope," he agreed. "Nothing."

And then we stopped talking and got down to the business of making love. He bounced me on his cock, long, hard, unrelenting strokes that were cushioned by nothing but his hands kneading my ass. I was screaming, there was no other word for it, my voice echoing off the kitchen walls, vaguely aware that the neighbors might be able to hear me since the windows were open, but not caring at all. Not caring about anything except this moment and this man. My life, my heart.

I felt like I was going to split apart, as if he wasn't just penetrating my body, but slicing through layers of emotion to get to the heart of me. I felt tears sting my eyes and I tried to blink them away. He pulled back and stared at me, his steady gray-blue eyes seeing into me the way they always had.

"You're okay," he said, and it wasn't a question. "I've got you."

I knew he meant more than physically, more than this moment. I nodded and clung tighter to him. "Yes," I breathed against his mouth, kissing him hard.

There were no other words that needed to be said. Just that. Just "Yes." Yes to it all, to the good and the bad and the messiness of loving. I felt another orgasm building and I gyrated on his erection, letting him feel every ripple of my pussy. He groaned and rubbed his stubbled jaw along the curve of my neck, nipping at my earlobe as he thrust into me, my lower back pressed against the edge of the counter, my head thrown back as I tightened on him and came. And that was all it took for him. He let out a groan to rival my screams, filling me with a flood of wetness to rival the puddle I'd left on the counter.

I clung to him, licking and biting his shoulder, digging my nails into his back as we rode out our mutual orgasms. I felt his thigh muscles quiver as he slipped from me and slowly lowered me down his body until I was standing pressed against him, our bodies damp and flushed. We held each other for a long time, until the sweat cooling on my body made me shiver and my breathing had returned to normal. I tilted my head to look at him, feeling as if I was seeing him for the first time.

"Wow," was all I could manage.

He laughed. "Wow, indeed."

I didn't know what else to say. I could feel the walls rebuilding, could feel us retreating to our mutual corners. I grabbed him by the upper arms, feeling the flex of his biceps, and shook him.

"Let's not lose this," I demanded fiercely. "Let's never lose this again."

He twisted his fingers in my hair and tugged, until my neck arched and my mouth tilted up to the right angle for him to kiss me.

"We never lost it," he murmured against my mouth. "We just forgot it."

I couldn't argue. "So let's not forget. Keep reminding me. I'll keep reminding you. Nothing can break us," I said, my voice vibrating with the intensity of my emotion the way my body had been humming with the intensity of sensation just a few moments earlier.

"I'll remind you. Again and again," he promised.

"Good. Remind me again in about six hours when this party is behind us."

"Oh, yeah," he said, bending to retrieve my forgotten towel. "Your mom will be back with the boys soon. Ready to celebrate?"

"I think we just did."

I gave him a wink and smile before turning on my heel and padding naked down the hall, but not before catching a glimpse of his surprised, appreciative expression. We were going to be okay. I was sure of it.

ABOUT THE AUTHORS

VICTORIA BLISSE is a mother, wife, Christian and Manchester United Fan who loves to create stories and poems. Born near Manchester, England, her northern English quirkiness shows through in her stories. Passion, love and laughter fill her work, just as they fill her life.

HEIDI CHAMPA (heidichampa.blogspot.com) has been published in numerous anthologies including *Best Women's Erotica 2010, Playing With Fire, Frenzy* and *Ultimate Curves*. She has also steamed up the pages of *Bust* Magazine. In electronic form, she can be found at Clean Sheets, Ravenous Romance, Oysters and Chocolate and The Erotic Woman.

EROBINTICA is poet, writer and blogger Robin Elizabeth Sampson. Her erotica's been included in *Coming Together: Al Fresco, Best Erotic Romance* and *Suite Encounters: Hotel Sex Stories*. Two of her poems were finalists at the 2010 Seattle

Erotic Art Festival and she's featured at Philadelphia's The Erotic Literary Salon.

After brief, unsatisfying careers in advertising, teaching, computers and homemaking, **JEANETTE GREY** has returned to her two first loves: romance and writing. She lives in North Carolina with her husband and pet frog.

A. M. HARTNETT (amhartnett.com) published her first erotic short in 2006 and since then her work has appeared in numerous anthologies, including Cleis Press's *Passion: Erotic Romance for Women* (2010) and *Going Down: Oral Sex Stories* (2012).

CRYSTAL JORDAN is originally from California, but has lived all over the United States. Currently, she serves as a librarian at a university in her home state, and she writes paranormal, contemporary, futuristic, and erotic romance. Her publishers include Kensington Aphrodisia, Harlequin Spice Briefs, Ellora's Cave, and Samhain Publishing.

GENEVA KING (genevaking.com) has stories appearing in over a dozen anthologies including: *Best Women's Erotica 2006, Ultimate Lesbian Erotica 2009, Ultimate Undies, Caramel Flava, Peep Show* and *Travelrotica for Lesbians 1 & 2.*

KRISTINA LLOYD (kristinalloyd.co.uk) is the author of three erotic novels including the controversial *Asking for Trouble.* Her short stories have appeared in numerous anthologies and her work has been translated into German, Dutch and Japanese. She has a master's degree in Twentieth Century Literature and lives in Brighton, UK.

NIKKI MAGENNIS (nikkimagennis.com) is an author and artist. She has written two novels and dozens of short stories, and is mostly a home bird, although she often dreams of flight. She lives in Scotland.

CATHERINE PAULSSEN's (catherinepaulssen.com) stories have been published by Cleis Press, Silver Publishing and Constable & Robinson.

Award winning writer **KATE PEARCE** was born into a large family of girls in England, and spent much of her childhood living very happily in a dream world. Kate is published by Signet Eclipse, Kensington, Ellora's Cave, Cleis Press, Carina Press and Virgin Black Lace/Cheek.

NINA REYES is a freelance writer, performing artist and painter who still blushes over the thought of writing erotica, despite the fact that she suspects she will do it for the rest of her life.

TERESA NOELLE ROBERTS writes romantic erotica and erotic romance for lusty romantics of all persuasions. Her short fiction has appeared in *Best of Best Women's Erotica 2*, *Best Bondage Erotica 2011*, *Orgasmic*, *Spanked*, *Playing with Fire* and other anthologies with similarly provocative titles. She writes erotic romance for Samhain and Phaze.

DOMINIC SANTI (dominicsanti@yahoo.com) is a former technical editor turned rogue whose stories have appeared in many dozens of publications, including *Best American Erotica*; *Hot Under the Collar*; *Surrender*; *Yes, Ma'am*; *Caught Looking*; *Sex and Candy*; *Voyeur Eyes Only—Vegas Windows*; *Backdoor Lover*; *Pleasure Me* and *Red Hot Erotica*.

TORRANCE SENÉ (dieromantic.com) delights in varied combinations of the erotic, romantic, horrific and speculative. When not writing, she can usually be found feeding her book addiction.

DONNA GEORGE STOREY (DonnaGeorgeStorey.com) is the author of *Amorous Woman*, a semiautobiographical erotic novel set in Japan, as well as over a hundred stories in such places as *Best Women's Erotic, Lustfully Ever After, Irresistible: Erotic Romance For Couples* and *The Mammoth Book of Best New Erotica*.

SASKIA WALKER (saskiawalker.co.uk) began writing in the late 1990s. She'd traveled the world, gained degrees in art history, literature and visual arts, and worked in several diverse careers, but the stories in her head needed to be written. Since then, she's penned a dozen novels and more than eighty short stories. She lives in the north of England with her real-life hero, Mark.

ABOUT THE EDITOR

Described by The Romance Reader as "a budding force to be reckoned with," **KRISTINA WRIGHT** (kristinawright.com) is a full-time writer and the editor of the bestselling *Fairy Tale Lust: Erotic Fantasies for Women,* as well as other Cleis Press anthologies including *Dream Lover: Paranormal Tales of Erotic Romance*; *Steamlust: Steampunk Erotic Romance*; *Lustfully Ever After: Fairy Tale Erotic Romance*; *Duty and Desire: Military Erotic Romance* and the *Best Erotic Romance* series. Kristina's erotica and erotic romance fiction has appeared in over one hundred anthologies and her articles, interviews and book reviews have appeared in numerous publications, both print and online. She received the Golden Heart Award for Romantic Suspense from Romance Writers of America for her first novel *Dangerous Curves* and she is a member of RWA as well as the special interest chapters Passionate Ink and Fantasy, Futuristic and Paranormal. She is a book reviewer for the Erotica Readers and Writers Association (erotica-readers.com) and blogs regularly at the multiauthor blog Oh Get a Grip! (ohgetagrip. blogspot.com). She holds degrees in English and humanities and has taught college composition and world mythology at the community college level. Originally from South Florida, Kristina is living happily ever after in Virginia with her husband Jay and their two little boys.